PROTECTION

Kenneth van Aswegen

 www.trafford.com

North America & international
toll-free: 1 888 232 4444 (USA & Canada)
phone: 250 383 6864 ♦ fax: 812 355 4082

High, Commander Alison brings his spacecraft in line with the mother ship in order to dock.

Suddenly there was an explosion in the mother ship so fierce that his craft was thrown out of its flight path.

Commander Alison immediately moved his craft away from the burning mother ship and stationed himself out of harms way, he tries to contact the ship but there came no response. Then as he expected the mother ship blew up into small pieces. "That is what always happens just as I need a break ". He thought to himself.

"This war must now really come to an end I am tired, my men are tired and our recourses are running very low." He said to himself as he turned his craft around and returned to base where he now has to fill in a lot of paper work on that incident.

On arriving at the base a lovely young girl came up to him and inform him that the admiral wanted to see him the moment he arrived, he thanked her and went straight to the Admiral's office, on arrival he saw that the Admiral was in an argument with someone he did not know in civilian clothing. The Admiral saw him and immediately called him in.

"Commander Alison, glad you are here," he was greeted. "This is Mr. Dunn from the Intergalactic command intelligence section and he claims that an assassination attempt was made on you today, what do you think of that?" ask the Admiral.

Commander Alison shakes hands with Mr. Dunn and then replies, "It depends on who's got a grudge against me, I do not know of any person who would be so low to kill two hundred people just to get to me!" "We received information that the enemy have put a price on your head as you and your men has made them to suffer heavy losses this last couple of months." said Mr. Dunn.

"That is because you changed your war pattern plus introduced new skills to fight the enemy, that confused them and hence your success, that also makes you the most wanted man in the universe." the Admiral replied.

"Now, my suggestion is that you and your men take a break and go home for a while, rest out and then when they think that you died in that explosion you come back and show them how dead you really are." says Mr. Dunn.

The Admiral instantly went red in his face from frustration, "That is what we were arguing about, you and your men are the best in the universe, and to lose you all so suddenly is going to cause major problems for this unit, but I have no option you and your men are on leave for a month effective immediately. No communication to any one about this or the fact that you are on leave. Am I understood Commander?" asks the Admiral.

"Loud and clear Admiral you know where to find Me." says the Commander.

"Yes, and send regards to Evelyn and your son for me will you?" says the Admiral.

"Ok" replied the Commander as he turned to leave. He was relieved that he got the break for himself and for his men, as they really deserve it.

Two weeks later, Evelyn decided to go and visit her mother and he did not want to go as he got some work to do, as because of the war he does not have time to repair the house and work in the garden any more. He watched her as she lifts up over the trees and was about to turn back into the house when suddenly the craft exploded in mid air and sent pieces flying towards him, he had to dive for cover, he then ran to where the craft was lying on its roof and he could clearly see that his wife and son did not survive the explosion.

The Admiral evacuated the Commander the moment he received the news of the death of the Commander's wife and child, and sent him to a remote location under heavy guard and security, which at that time the Commander did not understand what the reasons for it was. However, he knew that to argue would have no affect what so ever, so he just went along with the guards.

A Week later the Admiral arrived very suddenly and without warning like a ghost he just appeared
Out of thin air, this surprises the Commander and the guards.

"Commander Alison, sorry for the delay to come back to you and condolences for your loss my friend." said the Admiral.
"Thank you for assisting Admiral, but what the security is for?" ask the Commander.

"Do you remember Mr. Dunn that gay from Intergalactic command Inelegance?" ask the Admiral.

"Yes what about him?" ask the Commander

"He disappeared a day before the your craft exploded, so we looked through his papers and found that he was a spy for the enemy and that he was responsible for your wife and son's death. So by the way, the explosion was set of remotely, but the person who did it could not see that you were not on board. So we reported that you and your family have died in the explosion," said the Admiral.

"Now what about my family's body's?" ask the Commander

"You know, the person who builds the bomb for your craft used so much titanium that no bodies could be found, only bits and pieces, we actually found only your wife's finger and an ear of either your son or your wife. Sorry I did not mean to upset you but we did not tell anybody of this and we have arranged your funeral for this afternoon, I would like you to attend your funeral with Me.," says the Admiral.

"Attend my own funeral, Admiral that is a sure way of telling any one who knows me that I am still alive.," said the Commander.

"Do not be concerned Commander, did you ever heard of a gay with the name camo?" ask the Admiral.

"No who is he?" ask the Commander.

"He is the best make up artist in the galaxy and he is going to transform you into someone else completely, I would like to see who is attending and why, the whole thing is going to be recorded, Each person present is going to be asked to say something to honor you, the reason for this is simple, we intercepted a conversation between Dunn and someone that apparently knows you well and we want to listen to the recording, and find a match. Are you on or off?" ask the Admiral

"Definitely on, just one thing Admiral, what was the conversation about?" ask the Commander.

"Not important right now you can listen to the recording yourself after the funeral, now we need to go, and to go fast." says the Admiral.

The funeral service was very interesting , his whole crew was there and it really looked like they thought that he really died when he asked the Admiral he was told that they did not know that he survived the explosion, he then saw one of his crew were missing , it was communication officer of his crew his name was Jerry.

"I Wonder were is Jerry my comunication officer?" ask the Commander

"We arrested him this morning, he wanted to confirm with that doomed mother ship that you are in the process of docking just before the ship exploded, we think there is a connection between him and Mr. Dunn, we are not sure where what and how but we are going to find out. Says the Admiral.

The camouflage was done very good it did not feel uncomfortable at all and nobody recognized him what so ever, he actually said something about himself in the microphone like everyone else did.

After the funeral, they went to the base that is located on an asteroid that just glide trough space, in reality this asteroid can be controlled to change direction to stop or to speed up exactly like one of our mother ships. One hundred and fifty personnel work and stay on this asteroid and very little people know of its existence, it is mainly use for intelligence work as it can go through enemy lines without them taking notice of it at all.

"Now the Admiral said you have two options, you can change your face and take on a new crew, or you can resign and take your chances to survive, the choice is yours what will it be?"

"The fleet is my life Admiral, how can I desert the fleet and run away like a criminal, or like a child that is scared of the thunder hiding under the beds. The enemy has taken to much away from me sir I cannot allow them to destroy my career as well. I will take the new identity anytime and the hell with it anyway," replied the Commander

"That is what I hoped you would say Commander. Now I took the liberty of arranging the plastic surgeon, and he is waiting down the wall for you everything is ready for you," said the Admiral.

"Let us do it Admiral I can not wait to get back into action again," says the Commander.

Some weeks later a mother ship was on its way to a space station five light years from planet Venus when the radar picked up an unidentified craft traveling at high speed on an intercepting course with the mother ship, the radio operator immediately tries to contact the craft but could not get any response. As the mother ship was continuously attack before and they lost many men including the commander of the ship, they are on edge, sounded red alert, and scramble their fighters immediately.

Commander Steve Holt who was piloting the craft was fiddling with the radio buttons to select the correct frequency for the mother ship, as they are unaware of his visit to them, at that moment his screen light up and he saw five fighters coming down on him. Commander Holt gave the fleet signal and stopped his craft in mid space.

The flight commander got the signal and ordered his fighters on green alert as they approached the Commander's craft, at that moment Commander Holt got the right frequency and asked,

"Would you be so kind to escort me to your ship as it can be lonely in space if you hang around here alone for a long time?"

Immediately there was a bit of a surprised answer, "only if you identify yourself properly and state the nature of your business."

"All right, this is High Commander Steve Holt from the Intergalactic command and my business is to asses your situation, will that be ok with you?" The Commander replied.

"This is major Kick, please lead the way we are your escort, and welcome here with us Commander." came the reply.

After docking Steve could see the running around in the mother ship as the upper command prepares to meet with him, they are in for a surprise he thought.

After the initial greetings some of them he knows very well but nobody knows him as he is in actual fact Alison just camouflaged, he asked the ship's Number one if there is quarters available as he is going to stay over a few days.

"Certainly Commander, the previous Commanders quarters are empty as he did not make the last attack, rest his soul," says the Number one "Thank you, I do know the location of the cabin, can you arrange a meeting with all officers at 19h00 hours today? And I will meet you on the bridge in one hour, thank you Number one." says Steve

Steve rearrange the cabin as he liked it and in doing so made the cabin his. Then he took a walk through the ship and notice that two security guards are following him where ever he goes, "That must have been the orders from the Number one, he then decided not to provoke them but if he did not have to meet with the Number one in a few minutes it would have been a different story as he feels like making some trouble in mischief. Especially with security, they are his favorite subjects.

As Steve arrives on the bridge, they were in visual of the space station and were getting ready to dock. Steve greed the Number one and study the space station carefully, then suddenly he said to the Number one "abort docking and change course to 10-19-15 on the double, RED ALERT."

The Number one gave the order and then looked at the Commander question as the ship needs urgent repairs, and the course the Commander gave is right in the middle of enemy territory.

"I know you are baffled but that space station has been taken over by the enemy and we were sitting ducks, we will soon attack the station, but

first we must talk. To the boardroom if you would please Number one?"
ask Steve.

When they arrived at the boardroom Steve asked the Number one to
remove the guards that were shadowing them from earshot, commands
were given, and the guards disappeared.

"Now, no one what is your first name, we were not properly introduced
yet." ask the Commander.

"My first name is Lucky Radebe and I am from planet Earth, but where are
you from Commander nobody knows about you, I have tried to get some
confirmation on your visit, but head office just told me to wait, they will let
me know and I am sure that you will understand that we are very unsure
of you, especially after the space station incident," says the Number one

"Before I answer you Lucky, you can give the yellow alert now we are not
followed but you can never be to sure," says Steve.

A Few orders were given in a telephone in the boardroom.

"Now Lucky let me first ask you where on planet earth are you coming
from?" ask Steve.
"South Africa, the only country that survived the third world war and
escaped nuclear explosions, sir." answers Lucy.

"You were very fortunate Lucky, and I myself came from Piran one of the
Palladian group of planets, and I was operating from there mostly that is
why nobody in this ship has heard of me before." say Steve.

"That explain that one, but what happened at the space station Commander I am totally baffled how you can know that it has been taken over by the enemy?" ask Lucky.

"Have you ever looked at the top of a space station? If you did, you would see a blue light and an orange light, if the orange light were out that means that the commander of the station realized that there is a problem and he does not want you to dock.

Only the commander of the station knows where to deactivate that light, and I received some information that the enemy was active in this area two day's before. So by the way only Commanders and their first officers are to know this information, that is why you did not know about it.," says Steve.

"Now that makes sense, what happens now, my orders was to report to the space station and wait for new orders," says Lucky.

"Would you like me to confirm that I am genuine before you worry too much?" ask Steve.

"If you could Commander that would really help." answers Lucky.

Steve took out of his pocket a disk for the main computer of the ship and slot it into the computer, he then activate it with a secret code.

"Only High commanders have these computer disks but this one is different as it contains a message to you from the admiral himself." Said Steve

With that, the computer screen light up, the admiral appeared on the screen and gave his message to the Number one of the ship putting Steve in full command of the ship, and with a blessing, the disk ends.

"Welcome on board Commander." The Number one said with a satisfied look on his face.

"Thank you, it is time to meet with the other officers in the boardroom," said the Commander.

When they arrived at the boardroom all the officers are already waiting very quietly, the commander could feel the tension in the room as they entered.

The Number one took the stand and immediately jump on the officers for not saluting a high commander when he comes into the room. One of the majors jumps up and shouted on the top of his lungs "officer on the deck!' Then, every officer in the room jumped up and saluted the high commander.

Steve saluted back and told them to be at ease, they took their places again, but the tension was gone and he could see some smiles here and there.

"The Admiral saw that we have a few problems and that our Commander does not exist anymore, therefore he has sent us High Commander Steve Holt to replace our expired commander and to get us ready for real battles against our enemy." said Lucky

Steve took the stand and all he said was "I Am glad to be here, there is only one order I have got for you and that is that by o seven hundred hours tomorrow morning I want a full status report from each one of you for your departments.

You must state what repairs must be made and if the material are available in the store or not, also state if you do need personnel and if you have excess personnel then state that as well. We will have a meeting again at o ten hundred hours tomorrow morning. Thank you and God bless." He could hear a few thank you would and God blessings as he left the room.

"You a man of few words." said Lucky to the commander as they entered the bridge.

After the introduction on the bridge the Commander told them that in the early morning hours they would cross the path of an asteroid, he want them to "hide" the ship next to the asteroid so that repairs can be done to the ship and under no circumstances may any crew member leave the ship. He then asked that the crew wake him when the asteroid is in view.

He was in his quarters when there was a soft knock on the door; it was a beautiful Clark that brought him the personnel files that he requested earlier on.

He thanked her and starts to go trough the files. It was just after midnight that he came to a file of an engineer and the photo of the member is defiantly Mr. Dunn from Inter Galactic Command Intelligence, the spy who just disappeared. Now he is working in engineering, interesting thought Steve, he better let the Admiral know.

Early the next morning he was woken up by Lucky, "we are approaching the asteroid sir," said Lucky.

"How long before we get there?" ask Steve

"In about one hour sir." Lucky answered.

"Good, can you tell me when this engineer came on board this ship." ask Steve and hand the file to Lucky.

Lucky studied the file carefully and then remembered. "He came on board about two weeks ago with a supply ship from titan , he said that command has sent him as we lost personnel in engineering and he is a replacement. Why sir?"

I Know the man from somewhere but I can't put my finger on it yet but it will come back to me, now did you receive a message that this man is transferred here?" ask Steve.

"NO, I did not I did ask the operator to request the relevant information but I got pre occupied and did not follow it up yet sir. Answered Lucky.

"That would be interesting to see what head office has to say on this fellow, we will check up on that later. Let us have some breakfast first. "Said the Commander.

Later, on the bridge, they moved into position next to the asteroid and Steve made sure that they could not be seen by anyone. Then he gave the crew off to go and sleep. All personnel on duty by ten that will give them a total of four hours rest before they start repairing the ship.

Suddenly he found only himself and Lucky standing on the bridge.

"I Want you to get some rest as well Lucky it was a rough time for you these couple of months that just went past and it is not going to be easy in the future either." says the Commander.

As soon as he has gone Steve got the admiral on the screen and reported that Mr. Dunn is on the ship as an engineer, and what he wants Steve to do about Dunn.

"Beam him by accident into the asteroid, where we will be waiting for him, it is as simple as that, do you have the material shortages for me yet? "Ask the Admiral

"I have only what the store gave me earlier on, the officer's reports I will have in three hours time.
Do you want me to sent that report through to you now sir and then the rest can follow?" asked Steve

"Yes sent it now and we will beam whatever up to you in transport bay four.' says the Admiral.

Steve sent the report and a hour later he got the report that the requested articles was sent to bay four, Steve then went down to bay four and there it was , everything on the list was sent trough it is going to take the crew two days to move all the equipment that they have received.

Steve made the decision to wake the store officer up, and asked him to meet him on the double in transport bay four.

A few minutes later an elderly man came running into the bay, not seeing Steve's rank on his shoulders.

"Who the hell wake me up this time in the morning, "ask the store man angry

Steve then activates the lights in the bay to full and then the officer saw his rank and the bay that is full of crates and containers. He jump on attention and salute Steve,

"Sorry Commander I did not know it was you that phoned me, and what is this stuff here Commander?" he asks.

"You are forgiven this time, this is the items you requested last night, can you remember what you have ordered." asked the Commander.

"Yes, I do sir, but it will take head office two months to get the stuff to us here , that is if they have stock sir, most of these items are made on different planets and have to come to a central store and then only can it be sent out sir. So I do not know what this is sir," says the store man.

"I tell you what, you go through this and check your list that you gave me last night and then you come and tell me what is still short. I will be on the bridge." says Steve and walked off.

Steve then went to bay no six where he programmed the middle of the asteroid's position into the computer. He also programmed the computer to cancel the order, as soon as it was done.

As Steve got to the bridge there was already crew members busy working ,Lucky was one of them sitting on his behind on the floor repairing a damage control board. He jumped to attention when he saw the Commander and shouted

"Commander on the bridge" all crew members stood up and saluted him,

"As you were, "says the commander.

"Number one, will you please let that person that I spoke about this morning look at the transporter in bay five we had some problems with it this morning, what I want you to do is to transport him to bay six and then you must transport him back to bay five. He must have a look during transport if he can see anything unusual, especially in the transport back," says Steve

"Affirmative sir I am doing that immediately." says Lucky.

At that moment, the store master came to the commander and looked baffled.

"Commander, everything that I have ordered is here, there are actually some articles more sent that I did not requested sir. "Says the store master.

"Oh like what?" asked the commander.
"Like these key boards sir, 18 of them 3 big ones and the rest is smaller sir." says the store master.
"Good, can you bring the three big keyboards here to the bridge please, they are actually for me, thank you." says Steve.

"I Will bring them to you sir, but how did you get it right to get that equipment here so fast sir, I have tried that my life long but could not get it faster than the normal time sir?" ask the store master.

"I came prepared, I knew that the ship is going to need a lot of stuff, so I prepared myself and got the items beforehand.," says the Commander with a smile on his face.

"Now that's positive thinking," says the store master as he walked away.

The officers started to bring their lists of supplies they need in their departments to repair the ship; one of them is major Kick the pilot that escorted him to the mother ship.

"Good morning major did you have a good evening?" the commander required

"Yes, sir here is the list you wanted sir," says the major.

"Good, there is one thing I would like you to do for me please, in my craft is the flight data recorder, I had some trouble on the way here with some enemy crafts, but I did not have the time to analyze it yet, would you be so kind to analyze it for me and report to me, what you have found. I am in particular interested in the tactics that they used to try and shoot me down?" ask the Commander.

The major stood still and wide-eyed and look at the commander, he could not belief what the commander just told him, but he decided not to say anything until he looked at the recorder, all he need to know will be there.

"Certainly sir, I will do it immediately." says the major, and took of with speed that broad a smile on the commanders face.

Just then does the store master returned with the three keyboards, Steve smiled and without a word took one, and disconnect the weapon system and cast the controls aside, he then plucked in the keyboard. The crew stood with wide eyes and some with open hanging mouths. They could not belief what they are seeing is real, this in their minds are the ships defense mechanism and it is now useless. The Commander activates the system again and to their surprise, a completely new graphics appeared on the screen.

"How this new system does work Commander?" ask one of the crew members.

"Can you play a music instrument like these?" ask the commander.

"Yes, sir but not the way you connected it there." said the crew member

"Ok" "Now let us play a game here, would you like that?" asks the commander

"Yes." was heard from everyone on the bridge.

"Do you see that rock there, right you take laser no 1 and I am going to time you, shoot at the rock at your own time," says the commander.

The officer took the controls and circle the target first and then fired the laser, the rock shook but remained,

"Right it took you exactly one minute and thirty two seconds to frighten the rock," the commander said.

Then Steve took his keyboard, activate the laser then he activate his stopwatch, then he first made sure that everyone is watching, then he played a little song on the keyboard and the rock disintegrated into millions of pieces, then Steve stopped the watch. Exactly twenty four seconds. Impressed sounds were heard across the bridge.

"Now, can you see why the enemy could get to us so easy in the past, we had to catch them off guard in order to shoot them down, with this new system it is a different ball game, don't you agree?" ask the commander.

"Yes Sir" was heard across the bridge.

At that moment, the Number one came on the bridge, grey in the face he told the commander.

"We have a problem with the transporter in bay five as you said sir, I have lost that engineer, and I could not get him back, no matter what I do sir , I have tried everything sir." said Lucky

"That is no problem Number one, your engineer is safe I do now were he is, but we will discuss this at a later time," said the Commander.

Lucky gave a sigh of relieve as he does not like it when things go wrong, he is just glad that the commander is there to handle things the way he does it.

The computer kicks out three lists of items that are still short to repair the ship to full battle stage and Steve and the Number one look over them.
The first list is personnel shortages and in which departments they were short.

The second list is materials needed to repair the ship and to stock the store.

In addition, the third list is the one that alarmed Steve the most; it actually made him very angry right there on the spot.

"Let us go to the boardroom Number one!" demand Steve

Lucky could sense that in the tone of the Commanders voice that he is in trouble.

The Commander does not beat around the bush when they arrived at the boardroom.

"I See that the food supplies are dangerously low, there is just enough food to feed the crew for two meals, how could you allow this to happen Number one, this is part of life support and therefore threatening the ships survival in space?" ask the Commander angrily.

"The head chef died in one of the attacks sir and nobody checked the supplies sir, I did not even know that we are so short." explain Number one.

"It is your responsibility to take over the work of the head chef or to delegate someone to take over that department, you were thought that at officer training or did you forget?" ask the commander, he is now really getting hot under the collar, as he cannot tolerate this careless behavior of an senior officer.

"Sorry sir I was very preoccupied to get the ship to the space station." says the Number one.

"Well let us get the list to the Admiral and then work something out but from now on till we get supplies we are on emergency supplies only, the food will be strictly controlled." says the Commander.

With that, the Admiral came on line. "Commander Holt have you got the list of items that you need for me, I have head office down my neck for it?" ask the Admiral.

"Yes Admiral, there is three sheets of paper coming through to you right now, there is one item that really concerns me and that is the kitchen stock that is so low sir." said the Commander

The admiral studies the documents and then with a frown on his face said,
"How can this happen, Commander I want you to take disciplinary action immediately on the kitchen shortage, and I will see what I can do to help you out. There is a repair ship on the way to you now and will dock next to you in two day's time, they are just waiting for the lists before departure, they are fully equipped with technical personnel and they will take over the repairs of your ship, so that you can concentrate on the training of your crew." says the Admiral.

"Thank you sir, did you receive Mr. Dunn in one-piece sir?" ask the Commander.

"Yes thank you, the poor gay was so surprise he sang like a bird and told us everything we wanted to know, he wanted to know how did someone recognize him as according to the ships records nobody knows him." says the Admiral.

"So what did you tell him sir?" ask the commander.

"Not what he wanted to hear, but now commander tell me how long before you are ready for battle, that is now ship and crew?" ask the admiral.

"The ship should take at least two weeks to repair, and the new crew will also take about that long sir." answer Steve.

"No, far to long, the maximum I can give you is six days Commander, I would like you to have supper with me tonight and I will fill you in why, and Dunn was very precise on his facts we checked it out we are in for quite a battle. So I will see you then tonight Commander." Said the Admiral and he sign off.

The Number one is standing there with a very confused look on his face and does not have a clue what is going on.

"Commander, Help me out here, head office is two days away how can you have supper with the admiral tonight sir?" ask Lucky.

"Do not be concerned Lucky the Admiral is much closer than what you think. I am not allowed to tell you where he is now. Do you remember that engineer that you lost earlier today?" ask Steve

"Yes where is he?" ask Lucky.

"He was a spy for the enemy, his real name was Dunn and he use to work for head office intelligence, he caused a whole lot of death and destruction across the fleet.

The enemy was in need of one of our mother ships so that they could enter head office planetary environment so that they could blow head office up, and that was why he was on this ship so that he could make sure that you dock at the space station which now belongs to them." says Steve

"So I would have walked right into a trap, thank you for saving us Commander," says Lucky.

At that, moment there was a soft knock on the boardroom door.

Major kick came in the room with an unstoppable smile on his face. "Commander Can you please teach our pilots how to fight like that. You took out three enemy crafts within seconds, they did not even had a change to fire on you sir, I saw that they came from the back and from the sides, and normally they would have taken any of us out that way, but you showed them how to do it sir." says Kick

"You just had your first lesson major, and that is that nothing is impossible, I want to see all the pilots in the briefing room at 15hoo today for a training briefing, can you please arrange that major?" ask the Commander.

"Yes certainly sir I think they would be very surprised if you show them this sir," says the major.

"We will see you all at 15hoo major," says the Commander as he dismissed the major.

A while later a radio operator came to Steve and report that he must contact the Admiral immediately.

The Admirals face came on the screen. "Commander, I have arrange food supplies for you for two months that will be transferred to you into bay five as we speak, the repair ship will bring more stock for you, as you will be in space for almost a year or possibly longer, so please ensure that your crew pack it properly as much more is coming." says the Admiral.

"Thank you very much sir how are you doing on the crew shortage sir?" ask Steve

"No problem, there was a bit of a bust up with your old crew and the new commander could not work with most of them, he also rejected your way of fighting, and that is where the most upset came from, so you are receiving one hundred seventy five of you old crew back. Including your old Number one." says the Admiral.

"Now that will be only a pleasure sir, do you know who is coming sir?" ask the commander.

"Yes, a list of names will reach you shortly; they are arriving on the repair ship the day after tomorrow." says the Admiral.

"Now what about this Number one and other crewmembers that is then going to be in excess sir?" ask Steve.

"No problem we just sent them to head office for redeployment including Lucky Radebe. They can leave with the repair ship.," says the Admiral and sign off.

The list arrived shortly and Steve studied it very carefully, an emotion started to stir in him, he did not know that he still had emotions anymore after the death of Evelan and his son, but God it is good to be getting his old crew back, he now for the first time realized how much he missed them.

The next two days are going to go past much too slowly for Steve as he awaits the repair ship

At 15hoo, Steve walked into the briefing room, and was greeted with a sharp "Commander on the deck" from major Kick.

"As you were, "says the commander.

"Major Kick I trust that you showed the recording already, so I don't have to show it again?" ask the commander.

"Yes I did sir." says the major sheepishly.

"Good then fellows, for the next two days we are going to do evaluations on flying and tactical fighting skills, I would like to see who needs training more and who needs less, there is no such thing as a bad pilot or a bad fighter, it all boils down to training, you all saw the recording and that is the standard that I would like you all to be on, and that comes only with training.

Now as we are in enemy territory it is advisable to move out in small groups of ten at a time and the remaining pilots do the evaluation together with me, now that is a nice game to play, and that is all it really is, is a game the one who enjoys it the most is normally the one who wins.

We will meet again tomorrow morning at seven in full battle dress. Said Steve

"Number one can you make sure that all crafts are ready and fully bombed up?" ask the commander.

"Yes sir." says Lucky.

Steve returns to his room to prepare for his dinner with the Admiral.

Steve had to be careful when he transferred himself to the asteroid, as nobody must know of its existence, so he had to program the delete message into the computer again and then transferred himself into the asteroid.

The Admiral was dressed in civilian clothing which consist of denims and a t shirt with star travel shoes, "very comfortable outfit," thought Steve as they sit down to have something small to drink.

The Admiral congratulate Steve for the way he manage to transfer Dunn to him, Dunn still does not know were he is and what facility he is in as the interior of the asteroid is like a building inside with no windows and consist of a couple of floors with cabins like offices just more comfortable.

Of course, he did not see the rest of the facilities, like the bridge and the engineering departments, or the fighter squadrons that is below the quarters.

"Let me fill you in on the information that we received from Dunn." said the Admiral
"The enemy is planning to build up a big force one and a half light years from here, some of the force are already at the assembly point, we checked it out without being noticed and there is already more than thirty mother ships in the area." said the Admiral

They plan to be all in position by the end of this week and then they are going to attack all our strong holdings, from here to be our head office is located on planet Astoria.

Originally they thought of capturing your ship at the space station but you fooled them, in the meantime since you sent us the message we manage to recapture the station with one of our forces they did not know off." says the Admiral.

"Who was it that recapture the station?" ask Steve

"Oh it was the third legion of the planet Zeon, Yeah I thought you did not know that they were on our side; they actually joined forces with us after they were attacked by Barrack mercenary soldiers that formed part of our enemies. We actually found out from the Zion's that several of the Dakar group of planets are actually dying out and that is the reason they are at war with us as the Pleiades group of planets which includes Earth and Orion consist of all the minerals and life sustaining possibilities and they want it all for themselves, very selfish don't you think so commander?" ask the Admiral

"That is the way I know the Dakar sir, when I visited their planet many years ago I could sense that they are covert in many ways, and were hiding something but I could never put my finger on to anything, but now we know." said Steve.

"The force according to Dunn is going to consist of Five hundred ships of all kinds and sizes, from all the planets that they could form an allegiance with them." Said the Admiral

"Now what we did when we were in the area was to put in place sensors in the form of rock all around the assembly point

So that information can be transmitted to us as a ship passes the rock, the frequency we use is very low and weak and they most properly won't pick it up, what the sensors do is to take a photograph of the passing ship and transmit it to us here where it will be processed and then we can identify how many there are and how do they look like." Said the Admiral

"That will make identifying enemy ships much more effective as all our ships computers will be loaded with the information, can you now see why I can't give you more time to repair your ship?" ask the Admiral.

"Yes that makes it totally clear, where is Dunn now?" ask Steve.

"We shipped him out this afternoon to head quarters were he will stand trail, he should be there by tomorrow evening if everything goes well, the pilots have strict instructions to kill him if they are under attack by enemy forces as we cannot allow him to join them at this sensitive stage." says the Admiral.

"What defense actions are we planning to combat this new treat that we are facing Admiral?" ask Steve.

"You will lead an attack as soon as our other ships are in position, the final plans will only be available in the near future, upper command is worried that more spies like Dunn are among us and we do not want the enemy to know that we know their plans, also nobody is to know why they are to deploy in this area over the next few days, orders were already issued and six mother ships are to report here tomorrow." says the Admiral.

"Admiral I am planning to take my pilots and do an evaluation program over the next two days in the area, I do need to train the best of them as

I do not going to have enough pilots with only some of my crew returning I do need to keep some of the existing pilots. What area do you want me to operate in as I do not want anyone to see me operating and to start asking questions, specially my crew, I do not want them to see the other ships in the area." says Steve.

"Good point Steve, I tell you what, contacts me in the morning and let me work something out that will solve the problem." says the Admiral

With that they part company and Steve returned to his ship, only to find the Number one on the bridge trying to speculate with two other officers where the Admiral was as he could not see were the Commander transferred to, that made Steve's mind up to ship the Number one of the ship as soon as possible as he does not feel that he could trust him totally.

The next morning before Steve did anything he contacted the Admiral and informed him of the no one and the actions he wanted to take.

"Steve that is very well as the space station is moving to a position five light years from this position and are in need for a second in command, as the station is going to have all the medical and repair facilities for any of our ships that will need repair in the coming attack, I suggest you transfer him there immediately to take the post there. He will not suspect that you do not want him on your ship as you are getting your own Number one back today.," says the Admiral.

"That's an excellent idea Admiral, did you manage to get me an area to operate in sir?" ask Steve.

"Yes, your area is 201-5 that is south of our position and totally out of the way , I also need you to patrol that area in case the enemy stumble across us, at this time that will not be so good." says the Admiral and sign off.

Steve went to the bridge and started to work out the flight schedules for the day, and then he went for breakfast where he met with Lucky and Steve decided that this is a very good time to discuss with him the newly offered position.

"Lucky, it is good to see you here; I actually wanted to talk to you about something that will really excite you." says Steve.

"What will that be Commander?" ask Lucky.

"The space station is in desperate need of a second in command with the possibility of being promoted to full commander within a very short space of time, as the current commander was injured last month and are there only temporary while he is recuperating, then he is to take command of his ship again." Said Steve
"The question here is Lucky, are you interested in the position as, this could be the lucky break that you were waiting for, and if you are interested, then you must tell me now, as there is other Number one's also applying, as this is a prime position." Says the Commander.

"If I say yes, how sure are we that I will get it?" ask Lucky with excitement in his voice.

"You are aware of my contacts Lucky, it will take me two minutes and you are in, you can bet your life on that." says the Commander.

"I will go for it sir, but what about you and this ship?" ask Lucky.

"Do not be concerned Lucky there is someone with your rank that can't wait to work with me again, but I have told him that we must first offer you this position and if you don't take it then he will apply for the space station.," says the commander.

"In that case commander then I would love to take that position at the station." says Lucky.

"Good, then I will do the necessary arrangements, and well done with your decision Lucky." says the Commander

"I Also need you to pack your equipment now as the space station is within transfer range to us at this moment , if the word comes then you can transfer immediately." says the Commander.

"Thank you sir," says Lucky and leaves to go and pack his equipment. After breakfast, Steve went to lucky.

"The Admiral gave you the green light to transfer immediately to the space station as the station is just waiting for you before it moves away again out of transfer range.," says the Commander.

"You mean that I have got the position sir?" ask Lucky.

"Yes, but you must hurry." says the Commander.

"Thank you Commander, I am ready to leave right away sir. "Says lucky.

The commander shook hands with Lucy and wised him well, then he returned to the bridge and made contact with the space station to let them know that Lucky was on the way as their new second in command.

For Steve the day is to long as he waits for the repair ship with his crew to arrive, he selected four of the current pilots from the evaluation program they showed the right skill to be converted to the new weapon system, one of them was major Kick a man that Steve liked from the moment he met him, Steve's intuition told him that this is a future high commander in training, based on the decisions he made in the evaluation and the way he gave the orders to his men in a calm but determent manner, showed Steve the potential for promotion with improvement.

The other pilot that caught Steve's attention was captain Laxton, a tall lady with a IQ of over 140 and a whit that matched, she also showed that she can make decisions fast and with intuition and she also followed her instinct which is connected to emotions that only a woman can possessed.

That in it self was reminding Steve of Evelan as she also did her things that way, so independent and also so vulnerable, and then also so beautiful and that is one thing that captain laxton don't lack and that is beauty, as she is extremely pretty wit long blond hair and blue eyes.

The other two pilots both men showed that they can work independently and in groups and are comfortable to follow orders and have the skill to learn the new tactics.

It was late that afternoon that they saw on their radar the repair ship coming towards them from the north, and at the same time, they also saw enemy crafts approaching from the west of their position.

Steve immediately ordered red alert and scramble ten of the pilots to intercept the enemy before they could reach their position and report it to their head quarters.

Then Steve called the repair ship and spoke to the commander of the repair ship.

"Commander we are under attack, do not attempt to dock at this stage, is their any way for you to render us any assistance from the pilots that are on board?" ask Steve.

"Sure, the pilots here are very board and because they brought their own crafts with them I see no reason why not. As we are so close to you I will request that, they all scramble and that will give them the exercise they need. Says the repair ship's commander.

"Thank you sir, and let them make contact with me the moment they are in flight so that I can give them their orders." Says Steve with a smile, as he knows what is coming.

A few minutes later Steve's old Number one came on the air, "This is flight commander Dex I believe that you need assistance, how can we assist you sir?" ask Dex

"This is High commander Holt Your new O.C, what I want from you is to intercept the enemy at
the west from here, there is some crafts of ours in the area if you want to you can team up with them and show them how it is done, my suggestion as it is a mother ship of the enemy is to use the third symphony of Beethoven that will do the trick." says Steve.

There was a bit of a silence on the other end of the radio,
"Affirmative sir, we are engaging now." says a surprised Dex as this is exactly the way late commander Alison gave them there orders and something sounds very familiar here, but Dex can't decide what it is yet.

Steve saw them teaming up with each other and he hears on the radio how Dex gives the orders for the symphony positions and also give major kick orders to keep the back covered as he does not want any escapes, so basically anyone that Dex and his team can't get is Kick's responsibility.

Steve saw how the enemy mother ship spit out little craft to defend the mother ship and that is what Steve want it to do, as in the past the enemy gave them heavy losses as to the way they were thought to fight, but to show the pilots the new system it might be a wake up call for the upper command to train all the fleet in this manner, as no other pilot saw exactly how it is done before, this is the first time that any other saw what is going to happen and how.

Steve saw how Dex move in to attack and how one after one the enemy crafts disintegrate in space at the same time Dex's second in command took on the mother ship with his team and within seconds the mother ship exploded into space, leaving nothing for major Kick and his men to fight with.

Now that is the result that Steve wanted to create as he knows that the Admiral and his side kicks are watching every move and he just hoped that they get the picture bright and clear.

Steve watched the pilots returning to their ships and while he was watching them the Admiral came on the screen and said.

"That was quite a show Steve, can you come and see me immediately please there is something that we need to discuss, the repair ship has been ordered not to dock for at least an hour, so that we can do our talk first." says the Admiral.

A few minutes later Steve the Admiral and four others were sitting in the asteroid operations room.

"Steve I think that you have met the ops officers before so I am not going to introduce you all right now as we have no time to waste by that right now." says the Admiral.

"Yes we have met.," says Steve.

"Good , Now that attack was the most incredible show I and everyone in this room have ever seen, Steve can you please tell us how it works as our lasers are by far not so effective as yours what is your secret?" ask the Admiral with a few Yeah, Yeah from the others.

"Basically all that we have done was to put sound into the laser beam and when the laser travel at the speed of light it carries the sound with it as sound travels slower than light. Now when the laser hits the target it instantly heats up the metal and then the sound which was carried at the back of the laser hits the hot metal and shatters it to pieces, if the ship has shields on the laser can't get through as you all know, but if it carries sound the sound goes though and drag the laser with it, so in other words the shields have no effect on our attacks so far yet. Says Steve.

"No how long will it take to train the fleet this method, and how long will it take to convert our ships with the technology?" ask the Admiral

"So fast as each pilot can learn how to play the electric keyboard and in what position he is in the fight, the conversion on our ships will take three minutes each." said Steve

"Commander Can you explain to me what you mean by in what position he is in the fight?" ask one of the ops officers.

Steve drew on the board music notes for one of Beethoven's symphonies.

"The front ships takes on the small crafts of the enemy and they are playing the violin sounds into their lasers, the back crafts takes on the mother ships and they are playing the trumpet and drums into their lasers, You see the more dense the metal the heavier the music note, and their positions in this regard depends on the type of music that is played at that time as each music piece has it's own positions and when the pilot knows his music well then all he has to do is to find out his Position for that music piece, which gets practice and practice until it becomes second nature with the pilot, and to swap pilots around is also not a problem as they know their notes and what instrument they are playing. Says Steve

"How did you find all this information out commander?" ask one of the officers.

"As a child I had a big affinity for music and I know from experience that music high or very low notes can destroy glass and if heated up metal all I have done was to put the two together and tried it with my old crew and it was successful." says Steve.

"Steve I must say that I was impressed with the way your crew handled the enemy today, and I do not want you to be separated from them any longer I will order them to dock now and we will have further discussions later I must sent up a report to head office as we only got the results of your fights against the enemy but never saw you in action before now, I am sure that they would like to use you in this coming battle to the fullest extent." Said the Admiral

"Now Steve return to your ship and receive your crew but you must never let them know who you are they can guess all they want I do not care, your life and the successes of this operation depends on that." Says the Admiral.

A while later the repair ship docked next to Steve's ship, Steve was waiting impatiently on the bridge as he had ordered all the pilots to meet him in the boardroom as they arrive, now all he has to do is to wait for the orderly to call him and then he can make his way to the boardroom.

The reason he does this is to ensure that the pilots get respect for him as their commander. Steve was dressed in full decorating uniform that shows how many battles he has fought in and that alone should earn the respect he now needs so desperately, although he knew all of them well and fought many of these battles with them, they do not and must not know that.

The orderly came and knotted for Steve, he thanked her silently and walked over to the boardroom, he could hear the pilots nervously talking softly trough the walls of the boardroom, waiting for their new commander and he clearly hears a voice he immediately recognize as flight attendant Rupert Foin saying "I Wonder who he is as he knows our special commands very well."

Then he entered the room and someone shouted on the top of his lungs "Commander on the deck!" At once, everyone stood up and salute him.

"As you were." said Steve.

He looked over them in silence, and suddenly he is glad to see his old crewmembers, but he knows that he must not show it to much.

"Well done on your victory this morning, I sincerely hoped that the other crew members learned something from you. Welcome on board I am High commander Steve Holt and I want to use this opportunity to introduce you to your fellow crewmembers. This one here is Major Kick and the woman is Captain Laxton, the other one is Flight attendant Roz and Flight attendant Acron. They served with this ship for a while now. And then he surprised the crew by introducing them all by name to the existing crew and lastly but not least he said the new no 1 is Commander Dex he is a man with a history of finding the enemy and then plays with them like a cat plays with it's food before he eventually takes them out." says Steve.

The crew looked at amassment to Steve, how could he knows all this and how can he knows us by name and face, then Ruperd Foin asks

"Commander, how is it that you know so much of us and how did you known about what commands to give so accurately?"

"Commander Alison and myself were very good friends, we were at the academy together and I also assisted him in developing the new weapon system that you now operate, I also saw a great deal of video material that shows how you all clown around and I also studied your files, that is how I know that you Mr. Foin can't keep a woman they always leave you as you are crazy according to them." says Steve with a smile.

The boardroom burst with laughter at that last statement Steve has made and poor Ruberd sits there with a red face.

"Now said Steve, your quarters are ready for you and the household mother will take you there, I want two crafts patrolling in a 360' one light year from this position every thirty minutes until we are ready to move out as this is a war zone, Dex would you please work out a schedule and let the untrained pilots fly with trained pilots to get experience?" ask Steve.

"Gentleman and ladies before we go, just one golden rule, nobody fires anything into the asteroid at any time, as this is our protection and we do not want the enemy to pick up heat sources on it. and once again welcome on board see you tomorrow morning at nine o clock sharp in battle dress." said Steve.

"Number one can I see you in two hours time on the bridge with the schedule please we have a lot to discuss and to arrange?" ask Steve.
"Certainly sir, I must say the crews were not so exited for a very long time sir.," said Dex.
"I Am also exited, it is good to have you lot here." said Steve and left the boardroom.

Two hours later Steve met with Dex on the bridge and looked over the schedule that Dex has worked out, the first two crafts were ready to move out and Steve authorize them to leave on their patrol, with them were major Kick and kapt Laxton as passengers to observe the tactics they use to find the enemy.

Steve caught himself staring at her and saw the excitement on her face made her even more attractive than before, luckily she did not notice that he was looking at her and he wondered why he likes her so much.

Then he realized that it is more than just liking her very much and that concerns him a bit as that is not very healthy if a high commander falls in love with a crewmember.

Although not uncommon, it has happened in the past before and things worked out well, as long as it is not kept a secret thing and head office is made aware of the situation then it normally carries their blessing. but the danger is jealousy from other crew members as they think that because you are the highest ranking officer that you always gets the best and that can be fatal as they looses respect for you as their commander.

As he sends them off he wandered why is he thinking of that he is surly not really in love with her, he barely knows the woman, but she really wake things up in him.

Dex and Steve worked it out that it would take two hours to complete the patrol and leaving a half an hour apart there should be eight crafts is space around them at the same time witch covers a lot of space and can give a lot of protection for themselves and the astoid.
Like in the old days, Steve and Dex worked well together and Steve suddenly took a star map disc from his table and asked Dex to follow him, they went to Steve's quarters. As they got to his quarters, Dex thought that there is something familiar to this commander but he does not know what it is.

Steve put the disk in the ships computer and the star map screen that is fitted onto the back wall of Steve's room lit up and the map appeared brightly, Steve dimmed the lights of his room and commands the computer to soundproof the room. (Only the commander's room can be soundproofed).

"Now look, Said Steve to dex, we are here next to the asteroid, there is an enemy build up over here at the moment, they are planning to attack all the strong holdings that we have got at the moment, including our headquarters on planet Astoria.

The force is going to be a few hundred mother ships and battle ships from all over the universe strong, that is the reason why our ship is getting repaired so fast and in space, at this moment our mother ships are teaming up in this sector here to combat the enemy buildup, but we want them to complete their buildup first before we attack.
They should be ready by the end of this week. Do you get the picture?" ask Steve.

"Yes, but how do you know these entire things commander?" ask Dex.
"A Spy was caught amongst us and he revealed all the plans of the enemy, it very important that nobody knows about this until orders were to be issued, I know that I can trust you so that is why I tell you these things." says Steve.
"There is a space station 15 light years south west from here, there is currently 8 of our mother ships there to refuel and resting their crew in preparation for the battle that is coming but not even their commanders are aware of the situation at hand they just got their orders to report at the space station. Tomorrow a medical mother ship will dock there fully equip for any emergency, the repair ship is also to report there when it is finish here with us. Do you get the impact of what is going to happen by this weekend?" ask Steve.

"O ' Yes I do, it is also going to be terrible as the other ships of ours are not as advance as what we are." says Dex.
"Correct and that is where I am going to need your help, I need you to set up a training program to train every person on this ship our weapon system including commanders from other ships, you can use any of the

crew or all of them if need be. I will also help to train people where I can," Says Steve.

Dex whistles through his teeth,

"That is going to be tough but it can be done we just need someone that can play music and the game is on." Says Dex.

"Good, get a good nights rest and we will start tomorrow morning with the training program and not a word to anyone why we are training them just say that it is orders from upper command that is all." said Steve and then he was alone.

Steve ask the computer to give him all the data on Captain Laxton and then he started reading, she has been married before but her husband died two months ago in battle, she does have a little boy of two years old that stays with her parents in the Pleiades. She has been on the force for twelve years and ten years his junior. She is also a very easygoing person and fun to be with, only positive reports about her were written. To dam perfect thought Steve, if I do not watch out I may be in trouble.

That night Steve slept very bad as the workman that is repairing the ship were making a noise near his quarters he soundproofed his quarters but the computer was offline due to work on the damage cables, when he eventually fell asleep he had disturbing dreams and also dreamed about Evelan and his son, they were having a vacation on the mountains on one of the Palladian group of planets and he made passion fully love to her in a pond near some big green trees.

When Steve woke up he was not in a very good mood, slightly depressed and still very tired, so he went to the medical facility on the ship and asked the doctor for something to brighten him up as he did not have a good nights rest the doctor gave him a shot of vitamins as a hand full of tablets to drink through the day.

When Steve arrived on the bridge he felt much better and consulted with Dex about the patrols that went on right trough the night, every thing went smoothly and there were no problems, the only movement was one of our own mother ships that went to the space station, The Number one off that ship did ask them if they knew why all the fleet is to report to the space station and they replied that they do not know about it. That disturbs Steve a bit, as that could start rumors on the ship

That nobody can afford at this stage, he decided that it is time to contact the admiral on this matter, as it is almost 09h00 and time to have a meeting with the pilots he asked Dex to start the meeting and he will join them shortly there is just something he needs to handle right now. Dex looked at his Commander question as the commander always starts a meeting. Steve senses his thought and shook his head.

"It is very important that the crew does not know what is going to happen at this stage, what happened last night is a concern as negative talk can destroy moral between the crew,
I am going to get information from the admiral as he is to know what is happening and give advice as to how to handle the situation correctly."
Said Steve
"You see Dex that is why we have superiors and I will tab that line whenever I feel the need to, when you are in command you are never alone although it sometimes feel this way, there is always some superior that you can talk to when you are in doubt.
It is their job to help you in making the right decisions for the better running of the fleet and your ship " explain Stove.

"Aah, so that is where you learn to make the right decisions, I always wondered how is it that you always know what to do and when. Now I fully understand and I will be glad to start the meeting, it would be interesting to hear the answer to that saga sir.," says Dex.

A while later Steve arrived at the boardroom.
"Commander on the deck1" shouted Dex as Steve entered.
The crew stood up and saluted him.
"As you were." said Steve.
Dex took a seat next to Kick and waited as Steve activates the star map on the big screen.
"Good morning." says Steve.
"Morning sir." greed the crew
"Now you have wondered why the whole fleet is assembling at and near the space station, well here comes the answer, you as you sit here proofed a point in the attack you made on the enemy yesterday. That was the first time that upper command actually saw what we are made of.
Therefore we are to train the poor bastards that did not want to listen to us in the past." says Steve,

The crew burst out with laughter at the way Steve put it. Steve could see the impressed smile on Dex's face.
"I Do need six volunteers to go to the space station and train the pilots there and their commanders as well, and you do not take any nonsense from their commanders as we only have till Saturday to train them as you know it is already Tuesday today, the Admiral will brief the commanders of your coming as they do not have any idea why they are here at this moment, now who is volunteering?" ask Steve.
Nine hands immediately shot up in the air at the same time, and the words "me, me take me." was heard.

"I Tell you what why don't all Nine of you go, and Dex I would like you to go with them and take the two flight attendance with as well as they also need training, I will train major Kick and captain Loxton myself here." says Steve.

Steve saw how Captain Loxston gave a satisfied smile on her pretty face and he wandered what she was thinking as he could see that she did not take her eyes of him the whole time that he was there.

After the briefing Dex came to Steve. "The Admiral gave a very good reason for the gathering, nobody will suspect now what is about to happen." says Dex.

"Well just a pity the admiral was in a meeting and I could not speak with him, I did however left him a message of what I actually about to do." says Steve.

"Now I know why you are in the position you are in sir, you handled that very well, but is that not dangerous to jump over the admirals head like that sir?" ask Dex.

"Sometimes it is, but in this case the admiral did say that we must train the whole fleet and what better time than now, besides he will appreciate the initiative as that is what they expect from a commander." says Steve.

Just then an orderly Clark came to Steve and gave him a message from the admiral; Steve thanked her and read the message aloud for Dex. "Good thinking commander I will alert the fleet that your pilots are coming to kick their backsides, and they better listen well this time. Speak to you later." Signed Admiral Jonsen.

"Well I would be dammed, another plan works out well again." says Dex patting the commander on his shoulder.

Steve could only smile at Dex, that is one of his finer qualities that Steve appreciate so much, what Dex does not know is that after this battle he is due for a promotion to high commander himself, he has earned it and Steve made dam sure that the admiral knew that, at their last meeting Steve actually recommended that Dex take command of a mother ship into this battle, but the admiral first want to see what is going to happen.

He promised after the battle has been won that he will give it some serious thought.

A bit later Steve took major Kick out on a sortie and start the training on him , the major was fast to learn the new weapons and very soon he had it under the belt, with some practice with the rest of the crew he will be fine in battle.

Just after lunch, he met up with Captain Loxton and she looked him up and down and with a frown.

"Commander you look tired I will do the flying so that you can relax." said captain Loxton Steve was taken aback by her statement but did not argue as he did feel tired but also relaxed as the statement that she made showed him how much he needed someone to take care of him, and coming from her it is a compliment.

"Very well captain you have the helm." said Steve.

She pilots the craft out of the mother ship and took them to the general flying zone not much of a conversation was made between them at that stage.

Then suddenly Steve's radar went mad and he saw that three enemy craft is coming for them from the east. "Hand over controls captain we have a boogie at three o clock." Said Steve in a calm voice.

She did so and stare at disbelief at the radar, Steve realize that the captain were never in a real contact before alone in space, and most properly that is how her husband died as she was horrified. Steve put his hand on her shoulder to comfort her.

"Do not be afraid little one, they are no match for me, what I want you to do is to observe and learn as you will be faced with a similar situation soon." says Steve.

Steve activate the weapons and move the craft into the attacking position, and waited for the enemy to come and get him, when they were in range they slightly change course to flank him from both sides as he hoped that they will do.

Then he played a little song on the keyboard and the weapons fired, Steve immediately moved his craft ninety degrees to the north and stopped. All three the enemy crafts exploded where he was a few moments ago. All that was left was a few fragments of debris from their crafts,

"Wow." Is all she said?

Steve could see that she cannot believe what she just saw.

"Commander I would like to learn how to do that, right now, that was fantastic. My late husband died in the same situation and he was very good. I personally thought that we are not going to make it sir.," she said.

"Sorry about your husband, but with this new weapon you will see that we are not going to suffer such heavy losses than in the past, the tide has turned for the better for us as a fleet, you will now learn how to use the weapons and the tactics surrounding It.," said Steve

For the next four hours, she learned a lot about the weapon and how to use it but as she never played a music instrument before and it created problems for her so Steve had to make a decision.

"I think the best to do here is that I teach you how to play a music instrument first then it will be a piece of cake. If you are free tonight after supper you may come to my quarters and I will teach you music this is for your survival in battle that I am willing to give my spare time to teach you, will you come?" asked Steve.

"I Will be glad to sir." she replied with a smile

Later that night Steve had a shower and dressed casually in jeans and t shirt with star boots and around his neck was a necklace of an eagle flying up into the sky with the words.

"There is no Limit"

Engraved underneath the eagle's feet. Steve sat down and relaxed with a book and waited for Captain Loxston. At that moment, his phone screen lit up and the Admiral appeared on the screen.

"Commander how are you, we did not speak for a while?" ask the Admiral.

"Hallo, Admiral, yes it has been a while is it not, otherwise; I am fine." says Steve. At that, moment there was a soft knock on Steve's door.

"Admiral would you mind to hold on for a moment I really need to get that?" ask Steve.

"Sure commander." said the Admiral.

Steve went to the door and Captain Loxston were standing there dressed in tight ski pants with a narrow top that stretched over her perfect breasts and sandals. Steve could not help but to look twice, she is really very attractive.

"Captain Loxton please come in I am just busy on the phone have you ever met the Admiral before?" ask Steve.

"No, never, is he here?" she asks.

"He is on the phone come and I will introduce you to him.," says Steve.

"Admiral Jonson, please meet one of our pilots Captain Loxton, she is here tonight for music lessons." says Steve. The Admiral's eyes went up and down when she moved into view. "Captain Loxton please to meet with you, look well after this commander, he is the best we have." says the Admiral.

"I Will do so Admiral and I am pleased to meet with you sir." she said with the most beautiful smile on her face.

"Commander Can I speak with you in private please use you headphones?" ask the admiral.

Captain Loxton turned around and walked away from the screen and the admiral followed her with his eyes.

"We are now private sir.," says Steve.

"Good, she is quite a dish commander try and keep it in your pants, I know that if I was not married it would be difficult for me to resist, I do not want you to lose focus now commander." said the Admiral.

"I will try my best sir, "said Steve.

"We have a few problems that need our attention right now, one of our mother ships has run into another group of enemy ships bigger than the one that we are monitoring now it looks like the enemy is using two locations for assembling their forces. The mother ship lost half of its crew in the attempt to escape and is in desperate need for repairs, it is stationed at the space station at the moment, How long is the repairs still going to take on your ship commander?" ask the Admiral.

"This ship will only be ready by Friday afternoon sir, but if I may suggest sir is that we all move to the space station and then the repairs can continue on both ships." says Steve.

"I do not want all our eggs in one basket, that I have learned from our enemies today, what I think would be better is that the damage ship report to this position tomorrow morning for repairs, if it would not interfere with you to much Steve." says the Admiral

"That should be fine sir." says Steve.

"Very well then come and have breakfast with me in the morning and then we can go over some more details, there is much more to tell you." says the Admiral.
"I will be there sir.," says Steve and sign off.

When Steve turned around Captain Loxton was sitting on his bed looking at the photo of himself, Evelan and their son,
"Who is this commander?" she asks.

Steve looked at the photo and they luckily remembered that he changed his face after that photo was taken.
"That is late commander Alison and his family, very good friends of mine." answer Steve.
"Sorry to hear about their death , how did they die sir?" she asks with emotion in her voice.
"The craft they were using got blown up with a bomb with regards from our enemy, you see captain if you are a threat to our enemies they will not stop until you are taken out, that is the reason that we are kept on the one side away from everybody to repair this ship, as we are going to be the next nightmare for our enemies." says Steve.

Big eyed she looked at him and suddenly Steve knew that she was scared.

"Commander is there a big battle on the way, I have heard stories of a big build up of enemy ships in the area?" she asks.

"How did you get these stories captain ?" ask Steve softly and sat down next to her.

"When Dex and major kick were on patrol they run into the enemy ships, but Dex diverted away and they were not followed, Dex just said to Major Kick not to worry about it and not to talk about it either, as upper command is totally aware of what is going on." She said.

"We are not totally sure what they are planning but, we are getting ready to combat them, in that respect yes there might be a battle on our hands and that is why we need to get you ready so that you can survive this battle as I like you to much to loose you now." said Steve and he could not belief what he just said, but he knows that it came from his hart and that he meant every word.

"I Like you very much too Commander and I am scared." said Captain Loxton after a moment of silence.

"I Understand how you feel captain but, if you are properly prepared then you do not have to fear the enemy, in fact they will have to fear you." says Steve.

"It is not only for me that I am worried about but all the people in this war as this is a senseless war we don't even know why they attract us in the first place, and I do not know if I am ready to fight such a confused war.," says captain loxton with tears in her eyes.

Steve decided that it is true that upper command only recently discovered why we were attacked and that information was not made public to our forces as of yet, only he who is in a better position knows why and now would be not the right time to tell her the reason for the war, he will first have to clear that with the admiral in the morning.

"Captain all I can give you is a promise that if you feel that you are not ready to go into battle then I Promise you that I would not sent you in, you can help me on the bridge rather, sometimes I feel that I need someone there that I can trust." says Steve.

"Thank you commander, you certainly make me feel protected." says captain Loxton.

Steve stood up from the bed and took a computer disk out of his draw and slipped it into the computer, then he selected a program and pressed hold.
"Captain I would like you to make yourself comfortable on my bed, and put this headphones and visual equipment on your head it is time to learn how to play music in the real world." says Steve.

She smiled at him ever so sweetly and laid on his bed, he came over and placed the headphones on her ears and just before he place the visual equipment on her head he gave her a long soft kiss on her mouth, her response was wonderful, she kissed him back and trough her arms around him, he then slowly pulled back and looked at her with a smile on his face.

"You know the Admiral told me to keep it in my pants and I think that I must listen to him but, it is difficult for what I feel for you." says the commander.

"He is just jealous, it is also difficult for me as I feel the same about you commander." says Captain Loxton.

"Let us first teach you how to play music then we talk about our feelings captain. "Says Steve as he places the equipment on her head that cover her blue eyes.

Steve activate the program and saw how her body relaxes with the programming of the mind, and he knows that she would play music from tomorrow onwards like a professional, as this is the way he learned how to play music.

The next morning Steve woke up early with the smell of her perfume all over his body, she left two hours earlier after a very passionate night together, they could not help themselves when the programming was finished she took the visual equipment off and when he took of the headphones she just grabbed him and he could not help himself from that moment on. She did agree not to let anyone of the crew know what has happened to them and how they feel about each other.

After a long shower, Steve transferred to the asteroid and met with the Admiral for breakfast.

"Commander how was your evening?" ask the Admiral.
"Pretty good sir, there is a few things that I would like to discuss with you sir." says Steve

"Good, let's hear it commander.," says the Admiral.
"Rumor has it that there is a buildup of enemy ships in the area, and the crew are suspecting a battle coming, what do you advice more to tell them as one of our patrols run into them by mistake and they put two and two together as they are aware of our own force in the area?" ask Steve.
"Commander that is a good time for them to find that out as we are into the finals of planning our strategy and battle plan, I tell you what commander,

tell them the truth and then we have nothing to hide later on. But don't tell about what plans we are making as it do not exist yet." says the Admiral as there food arrived.

"Another thing sir, captain Loxton told me last night that this war is to her and to many others a senseless war as they do not know what the fight is all about, they do not know why we were attacked the first time, and they still do not know and I am afraid that our moral is going down if they do not know the truth sir, what is your suggestions in this regard?" ask Steve with concern.

"She got to you hey Steve, can't blame you she is very nice, I have read her files there is nothing to worry about." says the admiral with a smile

"Can't help it sir she does something to me, she wakes up which has been dead for a while." says Steve with a red face.

"Ha, ha I Thought so, it does not matter Steve you have that right as well, just keep it away from the crew for a while." says the Admiral.

"That has been arrange sir." says Steve

"To tell them the truth would not do any damage, I will also type up a memo and send it to the whole fleet to get to them today sometime, I will also add in some moral boosters like the new weapon structure that you now gave us." says the Admiral.

"That reminds me sir, here I developed an hand gun that works on the same system as our ships one, at a distance as big as five hundred meters you can take a craft out with this gun sir, I first thought about it when at home I was cutting through some steel and my laser saw broke so I Converted my laser gun and cut the steel faster and more accurate than with the laser." says Steve and hand the Admiral his copy of the gun plus a disk with all the data so that the armory section can build the gun.

"It is a nice gift Steve we must just be careful that the enemy don't get there hands on to this as then they can get our technology as well, so I am not going to sent this through until the battle is over ,but I will keep this one on me thank you Steve." says the Admiral.

"Now, that great force is a big concern as we have discovered that there is another force equal to the one nearest to us that will make it three forces of enemy ships in one sector , so upper command issued a warning that no craft may enter into the certain sectors where they are accumulating for our own safety they also asked the Pleiades group of planets which are your home force to assist in the coming battle, they have agreed as they themselves has been attacked a couple of times by our enemies, luckily not with casualties on their side as they also are superior in weapon systems." says the Admiral.

That damage mother ship is not coming to our position as originally planned there is another repair ship reaching the space station today and they will do the necessary repairs on that ship, The repair ship is to remain there for the duration of the battle and this repair ship will travel with us to do repairs on any ships that needs it. Upper command is sending pilots to guard the repair ship and will be stationed on the ship at all times." says the Admiral.
"That is good thinking as that will mean that damage ships can continue fighting while getting repaired.," said Steve.
"That is not all, that write up that you gave me on the new weapon system helped upper command to fit the whole fleet out with the new weapon and all crews should be trained by Thursday latest, your training manual

helped tremendously, and that put you in line for promotion to sit next to me as an Admiral after the battle, how does that sound Steve?" ask the Admiral

"Now that sounds good, what made them decide that I wonder?" ask Steve.

"Upper command saw that you acted in the interest of the fleet and in doing so you actually saved some lives and possibly planets as well, so well done Steve." says the Admiral.

"Thank you sir, If there is not anything more sir I need to get back to my ship as I do have a meeting with the pilots at nine sir." says Steve.
"No, that is fine for now, I will call you if there is any more developments that is important, I want to see all the High commanders here on the asteroid on Thursday evening for formal orders I will let them all know but you know now already, so see you on Thursday Steve." says the Admiral.

At nine o'clock, sharply Steve entered the meeting with the pilots and as he requested all other officers on board, his eyes lock on to captain Loxton and she gave him a warm knowing smile then it was time to begin.
"Good morning officers." greeted Steve. "
"Good morning sir." came from the officers.
"Some developments has happened since we last spoke, now the first thing that came up is that you all feel that this is a useless war we are fighting as we do not know why we are fighting and why we were attack the first time." says Steve.
"Yeah, Yeah. "some officers agreed.

"Now we did find out that the Dakar group of planets are actually dying out, what they are now doing is to attack other worlds that can sustain their people in order to occupy them all for themselves, our group of planets are ideally for them and that is why we are fighting these selfish bastards, to keep them away from our homes and our wives and children, it is our responsibility to keep our homes safe.

Do you all understand the reasons why we are at war?" ask Steve.

"Yes commander, now I am going to kick butt." says major kick and everyone cheered him in supporting his words.

"Now that we cleared that one up the next thing that you all need to know is that the Dakar went to all the planets that are supporting them together and they are assembling a massive force to attack us and our headquarters in planet Astoria, (Steve activate the star map and dimmed the lights.) There is about five hundred mother ships in this area from the enemy, then there is even a bigger force here in this area we do not know the details yet of exactly how big but that information is coming through as we speak, then there are another force equal to this first one here, so no pilot goes within two light years from this areas is that clearly understood?" ask Steve.

The pilots shook there heads in agreement, the boardroom is very quiet as every officer is listening intensely all with there own thoughts.

"We are not sure exactly when they plan to attack us, but you have realized that we are getting ready for what might be coming, our own forces has also been secretly accumulating and the good news is that all our ships are now converted to the new weapon system and all pilots and bridge personnel would be fully trained by this afternoon, and that is across the fleet, which in itself gives us the advantage over the enemy as they are unaware of this fact and therefore we are going to kick butt." says Steve with a smile.

The whole boardroom was cheering about the good news.

"Now as an incentive to our pilots and bridge personnel, the person who shoots down the most enemy crafts will win a million credits on his financial status and a month holiday at an location of his choice for himself his wife or husband or boyfriend, or whatever and children all expenses taken care off, compliments of the fleet." says Steve.

Again the board room burst out of it's seams as the officers scream and shouted some words were caught by Steve as (I am going to be called the hunter and score the most kills) When Steve eventually got back into controlled he had to catch his breath first as it took some shouting to calm everyone down from the excitement.

"Now this competition only starts when we get the OK from the Admiral and that would most properly be when we move out to combat the enemy, now as you know that there is plenty to go around for and the whole fleet is competing, I am confident that this ship is going to win as we got the most experience in the weapon system." says Steve and a whole lot of yeah, yeas were heard

"Now, the next thing I would like you all to do is to get back to your roots and get more spiritual as you all know that the enemy is creating a lot of insanity across our doorstep and therefore we need to concentrate on more spiritual matters, if there is anyone who is unsure what I mean or do not know how to do it, you are free to contact me or the doctor and we will assist you in that matter, as we have to win this battle spiritually first, then the actual fiscal war will be over soon and with much less casualties on our side." says Steve.

"Also the patrols that were going out until now will be cancelled from tonight at six only pilots that were to go out are on standby in your quarters if need be the bridge will scramble you. We have to limit our visibility here from now on. Major Kick I will see you at eleven and captain Loxton I will see you after lunch. That all for now God bless us all." says Steve and left the room.

Steve made a turn on the bridge and sent a message for the remaining crew at the space station to return immediately. Then he went to his quarters to rest and prepare for major Kick and his final lesson, he felt tired but he also felt good.

As he came close to his quarters he could hear music that is played and it is coming from his quarters, he enters his quarters very carefully to find captain Loxton sitting in front of the keyboard playing Mozart "the marriage of figeo" a very difficult piece to play and she is doing it expertly, he silently closed the door and soundproofed the room so that the music will not draw any attention.

Then he came from behind her and kissed her very passionately on the mouth, she stopped playing and turned around and trough her arms around him they stood like that for a while, then she pulled him to his bed and they made love until it was time for him to meet with Major Kick.

"Can I come and visit you tonight, I haven felt as well as this since before my husband died?' she asks.

"Sure why not , just make sure that you are not seen by the other crew members, I will let you know when I would be in my quarters, as I do not know how long I am going to be on the bridge," says Steve.

"That is fine I will be waiting for your call." she said.

"So by the way you play the keyboard fantastic." he said as he leaves the room. He could hear her laugh as the soundproof door closes on her.

The session with major Kick went smoothly and when Steve was happy that the major would be able to handle himself in combat he took the craft home and write out a competency for the major on the new weapon system. After lunch he took captain Lydia Loxton out for the training and it went extremely well.

Steve made her shoot at three different rocks at the same time and she did that perfectly and without hesitation, that was a quality that Steve saw in her when he was evaluating her at the beginning.

Just before she took the craft into the mother ship, she said to Steve
. "You know that you are an excellent instructor, in the past I never learned fast it took lots of practice and a lot of passions to get me to do things right, but with you from the beginning it was just a pleasure, maybe it is because I loved you from the moment I saw you, and now I love you even more."

"I do not know what to say to that Lydia, I think thank you will do, but I have a lot of other things to concentrate on at the same time, but I can honestly say that there is a big love for you somewhere in here, and only you can locate that.," says Steve with a smile.

"I would love to search for that in my own way. "Says Captain Lydia Loxton as she docked the craft.

Steve just finish writing her competency when there was a message from the admiral that he must come and see him immediately as something has come up that needs their urgent attention.

"Well I need to go and see the Admiral at once." says Steve to Lydia.

"Why is it that when there is a crises that the Admiral want to discuss it with you?" ask Lydia

"It is because I am getting promoted to Admiral soon, just after the battle.," says Steve.

There was a bit of silence, as she took the information in.

"You mean that I am in love with an Admiral ?" ask Lydia.

"Yes you could say so.," says Steve.

"That is wonderful, But I recon that I must keep this quiet ?" ask Lydia.

"Yes please, we do not want the crew to be jealous now would we?" ask Steve

"Yes, now go on I will see you later then." says Lydia.

Steve arrived in the asteroid as the Admiral and two Generals walked out of the meeting room.

"Commander I would like you to meet General White and General Ross from headcounters,

They have some news that you might be interested in.," says the Admiral.

After the initial greetings, they went back into the meeting room and snacks and hot drinks were served.

"The situation is as follows, some enemy ships has been lost without a trace and your crafts were in the area, that caused a panic into the enemy lines as they do not know what weapons we are using, this morning when your people were on their way from the space station to this position they met with six enemy craft, the battle that followed destroyed all enemy crafts and no losses to you commander.

The enemy mother ship was in the area but your crew did not peruse it and continued on with their traveling as if nothing has happened. the mother ship was from the planet Slaton which was friends of the Dakar for a couple of hundred years, needles to say commander, the panic that was broadcast to there other ships was good for us, they have decided to rather not fight us and therefore to join us against the Dakar in battle as they cannot withdraw and go home as the Dakar is holding their planet ransom." says General White.

"What deal did you make with them sir?" ask Steve.

"My, my the Admiral told us that you are a smart man but, I did not think that you will be this smart." says General Ross

"Well we have promised that we will go in and rescue their planet from the Dakar as soon as the battle has been won by us.," says General White.

"How many ships are there sir?" ask Steve.

"They have just under two hundred ships commander and as you know we only have one-handed and fifty ships left in the whole fleet, so this would be an advantage to us." says General White.

"What type of weapons do they have sir?" ask Steve.

"They have the normal laser and rockets that is guided Commander the rockets could have been a treat to us if we did not know about it, our intelligence people are right now getting all the information about the Dakar and associates of what there plans are and what weapons they have to fight us with." says General Ross.

"That information will reach us here tonight, Steve can I call you the moment it arrive as we need to do planning based on that information." ask the Admiral.

"Yes certainly sir I will then get some sleep as I did not sleep well last night, so that I could be fresh when you call sir." Said Steve.

"That is a good idea commander, I will see you then later Steve." says the Admiral with a smile and a naughty wink in his eye.

When Steve returned to the ship he found Dex on the bridge and one of the other bridge officers showing him the written material that the Admiral sent down to the fleet explaining the current situation.

"Dex I am glad you are back can I see you in the ops room as I have to tell you something?" ask Steve.

"Sure, and it sure is good to be back sir." says Dex

"Well done on the little battle you had on the way here, why did you not hit the mother ship as well?" ask Steve.

"How do you know about that sir? I did not tell anybody about that, and that is to far out you could not have seen it on your screens sir.," says Dex with a frown.

"I will tell you that soon I just need to know about that mother ship first Dex.," says Steve

"Well sir after the fight I saw the mother ship and I thought as there is a battle on the come it is good to scare them before a fight as then victory is easy, that is why I never went for it sir." says Dex.

Then Steve told him what happened and that they are now joining us against the Dakar.

"Also I need to get some sleep as the Admiral and I are going to work right through the night to plan our defense, would you please make sure that the bridge knows that those ships are now on our side should they see one?" ask Steve.

"Sure sir and sleep well I would not disturb you unless it is very important," says Dex.

Steve called Lydia, she came to his quarters, and they slept together until late that night when the phone rang and it was the Admiral.

"Slept well commander, Get here after your shower and let us boogie, I will order some food for us, as it is only the two of us tonight the Generals are sleeping, I actually preferred it that way." says the Admiral.

"I will be there soon sir." says Steve and rang off.

When Steve got out of the shower, Lydia woke up.

"What time is it Steve?" she ask.

"Just after midnight, I will see you at the meeting later in the morning, sleep well my love." says Steve and he kissed her softly.

Steve arrived at the asteroid shortly afterwards and met with the Admiral, the Admiral was dressed casually and so was Steve.

"Good morning Steve I am glad that you did not dressed up as we have a lot of thinking to do and with stiff uniforms on, it can irritate me after a while." says the Admiral.

"You are right about that one sir," said Steve as they entered the mess hall.

"Let me tell you first what the intelligence department fed through you us today, there are three big forces and the one closes to us, which is now the one with the five hundred mother ships is going to attack our space station on Sunday.

That will be the diversion they are looking for to attack our planet Astoria, where our headquarters are on Monday.

As they reason that all our ships is going to scramble to the space station to help and then the big force attack our headquarters. The third group of ships which were to be the group that decided to join us is no longer a treat to us, now what is your suggestions Steve?" ask the Admiral.

"Firstly Admiral I think that plan is brilliant, if we did not know about their plans we could have lost this war big time." says Steve.
"YeaH, I agree to that," says the Admiral.

"Secondly sir I think that the Dakar must not know yet that these other ships has joined us, then these other ships can leave for Astoria now with some of our ships in case they are playing the fool and are just a plan to get us of track and take Astoria for themselves, their target is to protect Astoria and to fight the Dakar when they are on there way, let's say five light years away.

Thirdly, sir, we must then attack the five hundred ships on Saturday and make sure that they are completely wipe out. "Says Steve.

"Why do I get the idea that you do not trust the Sliktons very much Steve?" ask the Admiral

"No, I don't, you know sir that if you are friends with a planet and have fixed trade agreements for years with them and you do know what that planets condition are, are you going to allow your planet to be held hostage by them, and will you join forces against the planet because you are scared of the opposition. I Do not think so sir, something smells here and I do not know what it is." says Steve.

"I Actually agree with you Steve that is why I like your proposal let us get them out of the way while we are doing our attacking and keep them under a watchful eye." says the Admiral.

"Right but I do think that we need a backup plan incase we are right with our feeling sir, what I do suggested is that Astoria forces deploy two light years away from their planet and keep their own guard, I also suggest that monitor stones be placed five light years around the planet, I know it is a lot of ground to cover but that will put us in direct view of what is happening in that area, if the big force is moving in we would be able to spot them ten light years before they reach Astoria and can forewarn the planet." says Steve.

"I Like the way you think Steve but I would say let us not only do it five light years but also place some ten and fifteen light years away but only in strategic places, so that any movement can be picked up by anyone of our forces." says the Admiral.

Steve agreed with the Admiral, they started to write the orders for Astoria, and the Sliktons, the Admiral selected ten mother ships to keep the Sliktons under supervision and to shoot to kill if any of them go out of line. They have to move into position within four hours.

"You know Steve we are now finish with our planning and all the orders have been written and executed, what worries me now is that rockets of the Sliktons, we do not have any defense on that yet, if they suddenly turned on us then we might have problems." says the Admiral

"Do not be to concerned sir, I have already thought of that and have invented something that will stop the rockets, it works the same as when an rock hits our shields it bounces off, I just modified it a bit, later in the morning we are going to test it on a rock and if it works then I will give it to you so that you can program it on the whole fleet sir." says Steve

"Excellent, Steve I did not know how to handle that, will you test is as soon as possible please I would feel much better if I know it works." says the Admiral and Steve could see that the Admiral is tired, he most properly did not have any sleep with the generals hanging around him the whole time.

"Sir I think that it is bed time for us now as it is almost six o clock and we could get another two hours sleep in before our meetings begin. "says Steve.
"Good night Steve and thank you for your help here tonight, contact you later when I am awake." said the Admiral.

When back in his quarters Steve saw that his bed is empty and made up and he decided to get strait into bed, he was waken up at eight o clock by Lydia's kisses as she came to see if he is back yet.
"How late did you come in?" she asks.'
"Just passed six, you look lovely this morning are you going on a date?" ask Steve jokingly as she is dressed in full battle dress with side arms and everything.

"No Dex gave an order that everyone must be ready and dressed to move out immediately if such an order should come, so that is what we all are going to be dressed, very fashionable isn't it commander?" she asks.
"It looks sexy on you I wonder how long it would take me to get you out of it using only my teeth?" ask Steve
She blushes

"To late now some other time, I have to get ready for the meeting and there is still things to do before hand." says Steve and got into the shower.

"Promise?" she asks.

"Promise." says Steve.

Steve met with Dex on the bridge and after greeting everybody, he took him one side.

"Dex I need you to take Major Kick and then place this remote controlled shielding on a piece of rock away from anyone, then I want you to activate it, here is the remote, then I want you to shoot a rocket to the rock in order to destroy it, if the shields stop the rock then I want you to shoot two rockets after another in quick intervals to the rock, if the rock still remains then shoot tree rockets quickly after another, if the rock still remains then the test was successful. And Dex if it failed or not, you must bring this unit back, if this falls into the enemy hands we are in trouble." says Steve.

Dex took the unit and studies it.

"Nice piece of work sir, who made it," asked Dex.

"Well I did, as we have to make sure that we do not get caught off guard I had to do something as I hate to think about losing any one of my crew members." says Steve.

"Do you mean that you do not trust our new friends?" asked Dex.

"No, I don't but I do not want to discuss it right now," says Steve.

"That is in order sir I do understand." says Dex and went off to find major Kick.

Then Steve did a complete check on all the ships computer functions as well as the backup computer, he made sure that the Sliktons are given the enemy signal as he believe that they must first proof themselves, to change it afterwards could cause a delay in which lives could be lost.

Then Steve went to the board room early and start to set up the star map and also the drawing board, some crew members came in and started to fill the room while he is busy setting it up.

Lydia came in with one of the other woman pilots and they sat together in the front of the room.

The room run out of space as all officers had to report for the meeting some of the officers Steve had not met yet as there are so many departments in the ship that Steve did not have the time to inspect them and some were still under repairs and were not accessible for crewmembers.

Then Dex came in and hand him the unit still in one piece.

"It passed the test one hundred present sir, I could not believe It." says Dex

"Good, do you know if all the officers are here?" ask Steve.

"No, Not all of them." says Dex.

"Good morning and welcome to this meeting." says Steve to the full board room.

"Good morning sir." is heard from the room.

"I have not met you all yet, therefore am High Commander Steve Holt and I am in command of this vessel and therefore your commander, this is the Number one of this vessel and he is Dex Grindling, and he is in the force already twenty years and a very capable commander, any problems or queries must be put to him directly as that is your chain of command." Says Steve.

"Now there is a spy in this ship and I just want to say to this spy that we are aware of you and it is just a matter of time before we catch you several traps have already been set of by you and all that remain is for us to identify you.

Now I will be in my quarters between two and two thirty, if you do not want to be arrested on the spot then come and see me at that time, as this will be your last chance to make things right for yourself and the fleet. what I am interested in is all the information that you have and I will not report you to my superiors till after the war, if you are willing to cooperate then you most properly won't even be reported at all, as I do happen to know that they keep some of their spy's families hostage then it is not entirely your fault, all I ask of you is to come and tell me I might just been able to help you." says Steve.

Steve saw that this information is new to Dex, he did not suspect anything, then again he is not wrong as this is a shot in the dark, Steve does not know if there is a spy under them or not, he is taking a chance just incase as he is not in the mood for surprises. Steve lock eyes with Lydia and she looked for a moment worried, then she gave him a warm smile.
"Now there is going to be a battle in the very near future and I want every officer to prepare their departments for this battle, if your department won't be ready before midnight tonight then I want you to report that to Dex or myself and that also covers the repairs that was promised to be completed today, if you are not completely satisfied with the repairs or the workmanship then please report it I myself and Dex will inspect the whole ship today and tomorrow." says Steve.

Steve went on to explain what their objective was but did not give any details of how it is going to be executed, for security reasons only.
After the meeting Steve send the unit through to the Admiral and the Admiral then upgraded all the fleet's ships with the new shielding, that is done from his computer and he just send a signal to all the ships and the mother ships computer then automatically upgrades itself and its fighters as well.

Steve was busy inspecting the ship when he received a message that the Admiral wants to see him urgently. Steve transferred himself to the asteroid without any delay.

"Steve good of you to come so fast, our sensors pick up a smallish ship going from one enemy ship to the other it stays there thirty minutes and then moves on to the next ship, have a look here on the monitor this is a recording we have made and I have fast forward it a bit to cut the delay out, see what you think about that. Says the Admiral. Steve looked at the recording but can not speculate what they are doing it looks like a repair ship that is going around inspecting and then fiddles with something on the starboard side of the mother ships then it goes inside the ship and stays there for twenty minutes and then comes out again and repeat it to the next ship.

"Beats me sir, I have not got a clue what they are doing but do we have any technical data on there ships because if we have then we can ascertain what sits on that spot in their mother ships." says Steve.
"No, we do not but I can ask Dunn maybe he knows, I will do that and then I will contact you." says the Admiral.
"I have done something on our meeting this morning that I want you to look at sir, I have done it so that we wont get a surprise from our enemies as I still have a uneasy feeling about the Sliktons sir. "says Steve and hand the Admiral a disc from this mornings meeting.
The Admiral looked at the beginning of the meeting and smiled.

"That is brilliant Steve, we will certainly keep our part of the bargain if the spy cooperate fully and are prepared to be a dual." says the Admiral
"What do you mean a dual sir?" ask Steve.

"A dual is a spy that converts to us and then spy for us in return and only gives through to the enemy what we give them and nothing else." says the Admiral.

"That is very clever sir, do we have any of those around as we do need them now?" ask Steve.

"Yes we just converted Dunn he is going to be placed into the space station to receive information there and only report what we give him to report, we had to teach him how to draw information out of the enemy without them realizing it." says the Admiral.

At 14h00 Steve went into his quarters and waited for any spy or spies to report. He made himself something to drink from his bar and looking at his bed missed Lydia's company but work first and play later. At twenty minutes passed two there was a soft knock on his door, it was Lydia, looking a bit offish.

"Lydia, what is wrong?" ask Steve as he kissed her on her cheek.

"I just want to let you know that I love you with my whole hart, I did not want it to happen this way but could not help myself, I fell hopelessly in love with you Steve." says Lydia

"That is great, but why are you so depressed about it then?" ask Steve.

"I am the spy you are looking for Steve," says Lydia and burst out in tears.

Steve had to sit down, the shock of her words left him powerless and speechless, and he did not expect it to be her, the new love in his life.

"Are you willing to cooperate with us and tell us everything that there is to know?" ask Steve with a broken voice as he is now very unsure of himself.

"Yes I am, I actually wanted to tell you about this the first day that we made love, but I was prevented from telling you," says Lydia.

Steve recovered a bit from the shock.

"Why are you spying against us Lydia, let me try to understand this as I will do everything to help you to get out of their grip, what do they have on you Lydia?" ask Steve and the anger is boiling up in him but he knows that, that will be the wrong thing to do now, he must just stay calm and get all the data.

"My late husband was a spy for them, he did it for financial reasons to support me and our son David, he then realized what they were up to and did not wanted to spy for them any more so they assassinated him, his death was not an accident as they arranged with him to meet with them at that point in space and they killed him on purpose. At the same time they kidnapped David our two year old son and told me I now has to spy for them or I will never see my son again and I will also be killed, so you see Steve I had no choice but to do what they say." says a crying Lydia.

"What information did they want from you my love?' ask Steve

"The new weapon system, they wanted to know how it works and they also wanted to have a copy of it to study, I told them how it works but I could not get them a copy of it yet as you prevented any ship to leave without your permission, they understood that but this morning something happened and I really need to talk to you about this." says Lydia.

"Tell me then." says Steve with could shivers running down his spine.
"They developed something that they are putting into their shields that stops the sound waves to go trough so our weapons are not going lo have any

effect on them, they also said to me that the Sliktons are still on their side and they are planning to attack us in the morning with the Sliktons and the major force,

They asked me if I would not mind to leave the ship in the night and join up with them as one of their commanders like me a lot and want to take me to his bed. I can then stay there till the fight is over," says Lydia.
"What did you answer them then/" ask Steve.
"I just told them that I do not want to join them or the commander in his bed as they are holding me under duress, they then told me that is correct I better do as they tell me or I don't see my son again, but I do know that that is a trap now that they know how to defeat us they do not need me anymore, they will use my body and then kill me." says Lydia.
"Where do they keep your son?" ask Steve.
"I do not know," says Lydia.
"If our weapons are not going to be elective against them then what will?" ask Steve.
"I am not sure but they are scared of rockets and they also mentioned that the Zions have weapons that they don't like as they took the space station very easily," says Lydia.

"Look, the Admiral knows about the deal and we will keep to the bargain, you have a very good reason why you did this and we will help you, I don't condemn you for this we have to figure a way around this. I have to let the Admiral know what is going on." says Steve.
"Steve I feel very insecure, can we make love please, I need to feel you right now?" ask Lydia.
"Sure." said Steve and they made love, it was not quite the same for Steve as he was worried about the safety of the fleet.

Steve called the admiral.

"Admiral we have problems, I have found a spy on board and we need to move quickly to avoid been totally wipe out by our enemies, what that little ship was doing is to program their shields to stop our sound waves, and they are going to attack us at this position tomorrow morning." says Steve.

"Who is your spy?" ask the Admiral.

"You won't believe it, it is Captain Loxton they are keeping her two year old son hostage, and she wants to cooperate with us and she wants us to help her get her son back," says Steve.

"Bring her here to me and let us see what we can do for her, I do not recall seeing on her records that she had a child." said the Admiral.

Steve asked her about it.

"That engineer that disappeared removed it from the records so that you will not suspect anything," she said.

"Were you two working together?" ask the Admiral.

"Not really he just told me to get really close to the commander in order to get the information the enemy wants. However, I did not plan to fall in love with the commander. "Says Lydia.

"Steve I think the two of you must come here now I will get rid of the generals, we do not want them around as they will want to shoot her." says the Admiral.

Steve and Lydia transported down to the asteroid, she does not know where they are as you can transport five light years away in an instant.

"Steve there is something that I need to tell you before we meet with the Admiral, and that is that according to my enemy contact that engineer put a bomb into engineering that can be activated remotely by them if they are one light year from us." says Lydia.

"Thank you for telling Me." says Steve.
Then they were in the Admiral's office and he wanted to know everything. After she told them, what she knows and what she told the enemy they fully understand why she had to do it.

"Admiral if I can make a suggestion, let the whole fleet move to the planet Astoria with speed, then we will have more time to sort this mess out, as we don't have a defense apart from the Zions against the Daracks any more, once there we could assist to defend Astoria as that is their goal." says Steve

"Good point Steve, what we shall do with this beautiful captain Steve shall we put her in jail until we get there or what?" ask the Admiral.
"No I do not think that she is going to be a treat to us any more sir, I will keep her with me to make sure nothing goes wrong." says Steve.
"Very well, I think that you two have a lot to work out between yourselves and I wish you well, I will not report you to the generals but if the enemy makes contact with you we need to know about it and we will work out an answer for them, we need to play for time here Captain, will you do that for us?" ask the Admiral.

"Yes sir, I really want to get out of this mess alive," says Lydia
"So do we." says the Admiral with a smile, as he to likes her for the person she is and he understand why Steve fell for her, if it were the other way around he himself might have fallen for her.

"Steve get your ship ready to move right now, I will issue the orders. I think it is better if we travel together as we can travel the same speed than I we will be just behind you, so that we can still transfer around," says the Admiral

When they returned to their ship, they went to Steve's quarters and after Steve soundproofed the room said. "Nobody is to know that you were spying for the enemy, is there any more spy's on this ship?" ask Steve.

"Not to my knowledge Steve." she says

"Let us go to the bridge I want you to work with me on the bridge so that you can see what is going on.

Steve first had to contact the repair ship that was still attach to them to break contact and order them to wait thirty minutes and then to follow them with the other ships that is coming through.

Then Steve took the ships intercom and said. "RED ALERT man all battle stations. Dex to the bridge." and then he gave the orders for planet Astoria.

"Helmsman full speed to Astoria take the shortest route," Ordered Steve

"Yes sir there is an astral belt in the way sir shall we go around it?" ask the helmsman

"No, we will go through it and path the way for the rest of the fleet that is following us," says Steve

Dex arrived on the bridge and took up his position behind Steve, Steve called him over.

"Dex there is a bomb in engineering I want you to go there with the bomb disposal people and find it, do not destroy it we might use it against our enemies, just make it safe, as it is to be set of remotely from our enemies." Says Steve.

"How do you know this and where are we going sir?" ask Dex

"There is not a lot of time now to explain it all but we did have a spy on board and our weapon system is now useless against our enemies, we are on our way to Astoria to defend the planet." says Steve.

"Is the rest of the fleet also coming sir?" ask Dex

"Yes, including the space station." says Steve.

"Now I feel better." says Dex and left for engineering.

"Lydia, how was your son taken?" ask Steve

"On his way to the care centre my parents that was taking care of him were stopped by two armed men and he was taken." says Lydia.

"You are from Astoria, did this happened on Astoria?" asked Steve

"Yes, it was in Tiladam the capital city." says Lydia.

Steve got the Admiral on the screen.

"Admiral Can you contact Dunn and ask him where he took her son to, I have a feeling that he is behind it?" ask Steve.

"Good thinking Steve I will do that, and the big section of the enemy fleet has moved into an attacking position to the place where we was, they obviously do not know that we are no longer there, the rest of the fleet is already past that point, if it was not for the information we might have been in trouble, fine thinking Steve." says the Admiral and broke contact.

Lydia looks at Steve with big eyes. "Do you think that my son is still in Astoria, and who is this Dunn that you were talking about?" ask Lydia.

"Dunn is that engineer that I transferred to the Admiral without him knowing it, and I do have a feeling that he is behind the kidnapping." says Steve.

"I will kill the bastard." says Lydia.

"If he release your son, then there is nothing to fear anymore, besides he is now working for us as a double spy, that is why I think that he will cooperate." says Steve.

Just then does the Admiral came on line.

"Steve I have spoken to Dunn the bomb is in cupboard no 112 in engineering and he did not have time to activate it yet, and you were right, he was the one who took her son, he is been looked after by relatives of his, when he heard that we caught her he said that he will arrange for her son to be taken back to her parents immediately." Said the Admiral

Lydia gave a sigh of relieve, Steve could see that she was really stressed about it.

"Thank you Admiral I would like to know when her son safely at home?" ask Steve.

"That will be done." says the Admiral and the screen went blank.

"Lydia, let us go to engineering and see what Dunn has done." says Steve.

They met with Dex in engineering and the bomb disposal officers were there as well pulling of panels searching for the bomb.

"Dex it is in cupboard no 112 and it is not activated yet." says Steve.

Dex gave him a confused look and then went to the cupboard and opened it, and there it was, after a close inspection Steve saw that the bomb was big and most properly the same kind that blew his wife and son to pieces, it is certainly big enough to blow this ship to pieces.

Steve turn to the bomb officer. "I want you to take this bomb and put it in a container and put it into transport bay no 7 ready to be transported, show me how to activate it first?" ask Steve.

"You activate it here by flipping this switch sir." says the officer. "Thank you, Dex would you please supervise this and then meet me in my quarters there is a lot that we need to discuss." says Steve.

Lydia and Steve went to his quarters and Steve activate the ships computer.

"Computer, look for any thing out of place on this ship and report." says Steve to the computer.

A moment later.

"Commander there is nothing found, all programs checked out and the only new order was from you and Admiral Jonsen to upgrade the shields." says the computer.

"Computer, if a sound barrier would be created in a enemy ship how can you make it nullified so that our weapons can work on them." ask Steve

There was a moment silence as the computer think this out. Lydia sit very stiff against Steve and rest her head on his shoulder, she was shivering softly.

"are you cold my love?" ask Steve.

"No, I just saw the impact of what I have done, it only dawn on me now." says Lydia.

Steve then knew that it is retarded shock that is hitting her now. He picked up the phone and spoke to the doctor.

"Can you please send a tranquilizer to my quarters as one of my female officers received shocking news and needs it urgently?" ask Steve.

"I will come over myself sir." says the doctor and hang up.

"Is that really necessary?' ask Lydia.

"Yes I do not want you to collapse now at this critical stage as the enemy might want to contact you, so by the way how do they contact you?" ask Steve.

She took out of her pocket a small round thing. With an ear plug and mouth piece.

"If they need to speak with me then this unit vibrates, then when I am alone I place the head phones into my ear and place the microphone here by my chess, then I pressed this button here and we can speak, but it has only a range of five light years so they have to come much closer to us to speak with me." said Lydia.

Dex Arrive at Steve's quarters together with the doctor and at the same time, the computer talked.

"Commander I have found a solution." says the computer.

"Hold, I will come back to you." says Steve

"Good after noon doctor, there is your patient but I still need her to continue with her duties so not to strong please." says Steve.

The doctor nodded and continues to exam and Lydia, he asked her to give him a urine sample and she disappeared into the bathroom, then he turned to Steve.

"Commander there is more wrong with her than what you thought, she came to me a week ago with stomach pain and I could not found what was wrong at that time but it looks like I might have something here would you mind if I took her to the hospital for further tests, and I will let you know what I have found." says the doctor.

"Yes, sure doctor but under no Circumstance must she be left alone, when you have done bring her back here immediately." says Steve.

The doctor looked startled but an order is an order and he will do so.

When Lydia came back with the sample, the doctor and she went to the hospital.

"Dex I would like to fill you in on the latest developments, Firstly we did find a spy under us and this spy can for security reasons not be identified, not even to you as this is strict orders from the Admiral. The situation is that the enemy knows how our weapons work and they developed a sound barrier in their shields so that our weapons are harmless to them. "Says Steve.

"That is bad, very bad." says Dex.

"That is not all, they were to attack us tomorrow morning with the big force at our location where we were, and because our weapons is harmless to them at this stage we would have been wiped out completely, that is the reason why we are moving back to Astoria." says Steve.

"That will give us some more time to prepare something to hit them with as that is their next target." says Dex.

"Correct, and the Sliktons were taking us for the fool, they were not genuine and are part of the big force that were to attack us, also we have loaded that rocket protector into our shields, that is the one that you tested. So the whole fleet is now covered against rockets as well." says Steve.

"That in it self is a bit of good news, now sir is there anything that we can do to make our weapons more effective?" ask Dex.

"I have ask the computer for a solution as I do not have one, and the computer said it found a solution, let us listen to the solution." says Steve.

At that moment, the phone rang and it was the doctor. "Commander Can you come down here there is something I need to show you?" ask the Doctor.

"On my way, doctor." said Steve.

"Dex I need to go down to the hospital can you please go to the bridge and take over from the major there as we are nearing the astral belt, I do need to know when we are one light year from it as you are going to need some help getting us through that at this speed as we are not slowing down." says Steve.

"Not slowing down! Sir that is suicide." express Dex.

"Done it a couple of times before and I am still here, and so are my ship and my crew, we can not waste any time the fleets survival depends on it , we are making an highway for the fleet, as they are right behind us now." says Steve.

"In that case sir I will let you know two light years from it I would like to see you do that,

Commander Alison did it twice and I can tell you it is nerve racking to see." says Dex.

Steve arrive at the hospital and found Lydia sleeping on a bed in a private consulting room.

"Commander we have found a device bedded in her stomach not bigger than a pea, but we are not sure what it is yet, must I continue and remove it?" ask the doctor.

"Is there any way to determine what it does without removing it?" ask Steve

"Not to my knowledge Sir." says the Doctor.

"Very well then you may go ahead doctor." says Steve.

"The other thing is that she is three days pregnant, do you want me to terminate the pregnancy sir?" ask the doctor.

The news shocked Steve, as he knows that the child is his.

"No, doctor that will be her decision, and I will discuss this matter with her after the operation, can you tell me why is she sleeping at the moment doctor." ask Steve.

"I had to sedate her as she had to swallow a camera to see what is in her stomach, but she will be fit for work again in thirty minutes after the operation with no side effects sir." says the doctor with a smile.

"Good, I will be in my quarters or on the bridge, sent the thing that you find to engineering for testing and let me know what it is." says Steve.

Steve went back to his quarters and asks the computer.

"Computer tell me now what have you found?"

"Commander if we shoot at their mother ships with a computer virus that I have designed, this virus would be picked up by their shields and it will corrupted the computer program that runs the shield, and the shield will collapse, the whole action will take twenty five seconds to happen, computer microchips could also be left in their flight path that will have the same effect as shooting it, would you like me to load the program and send it to the fleets computers?" ask the computer

"Yes, but also put in there an anti virus protection program in case they do the same to you." says Steve

"That has already been done sir." says the computer.

"Good, continue with the program." says Steve.

Steve's phone rang it was Dex.

"Sir we are now two light years away from the astral belt." says Dex.

"I am on my way." says Steve.

Steve got to the bridge, took position in front of his keyboard, and activates the weapon system.

Dex took his position onto his keyboard and also activate.

"Dex I want you to take the left to middle and I will take the right to middle, we have to go wide and high as the whole fleet has to go through." says Steve.

At that moment, the Admiral came on line.
"Steve are you going to slow down to make a path and can we assist you?" ask the Admiral.
"No, we are not slowing down and you can get what we missed sir. "Says Steve.
"Very well we are right behind you." says the Admiral.

Dex looked at Steve and is very puzzled.
"There are nothing behind us but a piece of rock." says Dex softly to himself just hard enough for Steve to hear him.
Steve looked at him and just said, "say not a word about that."

Dex looked at Steve and suddenly smiled.
"Bless his socks that is clever." says Dex.

Then they came within range of the astral belt and Steve and Dex started to play a song on the keyboards, rocks disintegrated all over and create a wide path for them to go through, the next layer of rocks were a bit thicker and the song took a little longer the helmsman had to bank sharply to the starboard to avoid collision with one of the rocks that were to big and did not break up right.

"That is one for the Admiral." says Steve as they went through.
Then there was a third layer of rocks not as thick as the first one but twice that wide, again the song was played and the rocks disappeared in front

of them leaving a path a quarter of a mile wide and a mile deep for the rest of the fleet to come through.

"Nice work Commander we only got one that you missed, now the fleet can come through easily." says the Admiral.

"That is good so can the enemy." says Steve.

"Is there anything we can do about that?" ask the Admiral.

"I don't know yet but I will give it some thought." says Steve.

Then the doctor phoned.

"Commander, the device that I removed out of Lydia is a tracker with a Dakar signature and it is active, what do you want me to do with it sir?" ask the doctor.

Steve suddenly had an idea.

"Doctor Can you arrange that a parcel of human waist be made up and placed into transport room five, and let me know when it is there?" ask Steve.

"Sure Commander I will do so, And Captain Loxton is been escorted to the bridge right now sir she is fine." says the doctor.

"Thank you doctor." says Steve

"Computer, can you make up five thousand of those microchips that will attack the enemy shields and have it ready in five minutes?" ask Steve.

"Yes, Commander it will be ready in two minutes and I will transport them to transport bay five sir." says the computer.

Then Steve contacted the Admiral.

"Admiral the solution has been found, Captain Loxton had an tracker with Dakar signature in her stomach and we are transporting it with some microchips that will corrupt the enemy shields into the astral belt about five to ten light years from here, that will make them think that we are hiding there and that will give us some more time." says Steve.

"Won't the enemy then know that we have found her out?" ask the Admiral.

"No, sir as we are putting the tracker in a bag full of human waist, so they will think that it came out naturally." says Steve.

"That is brilliant Commander, go ahead and we will talk later I am busy talking to head office right now for father actions on what to do now, and do not concern yourself I have explained the situation to them and your lady is safe they will not prosecute." says the Admiral.

"Thank you Admiral I appreciate that." says Steve and broke contact.

Lydia came on the bridge, walking slowly as the cut is still fresh but she is not in pain.

"Captain Loxton I am glad you could join us, there is one thing that you can do for me, do you see on the radar where we came through the astral belt?" ask Steve.

"Yes Commander I can see that, what do you want me to do?" ask Lydia with a smile on her face for the formality, but she knows why this is so, the crew must not know that they have a relationship at all.

"Captain I want you to look for a place where the astral belt is very thick specially the middle part about ten light years from where we came through, we are going to transfer your tracker to that position to fool the enemy how does this sound to you?" ask Steve.

"That sounds very good sir, and I have already found what you are looking for sir." she said.

Steve looked over her shoulder and saw fifteen light years from where they came through an asteroid bigger than the Admirals asteroid in the middle of the belt.

"That is just the spot I am looking for." says Steve.

"Computer can you lock on to that position?" ask Steve.

"Yes Commander I have locked on already and are ready to transport when you are ready sir." says the Computer.

Just then does the doctor phoned.

"Commander the package is ready for transport as you requested sir." says the Docket.

"Thank you Doctor." says Steve.

"Computer transfer now to lock on position the package and your micro chips." says Steve.

"Transfer complete sir." says the Computer

Then Steve had another thought.

"Computer did you duplicate that signal that the tracker was emitting?" ask Steve.

"Yes Sir I did." says the Computer.

"Is there any other person on this ship with such a signal? "Ask Steve.

"No sir, do you want a fleet search initiated?" ask the Computer.

"Yes, do a complete search and report back." says Steve.

"Dex I want all fighters loaded with rocket as well we are in for a big fight, and I want our pilots to be prepared, would you arrange that and supervise it by making regular checks on the technicians?" ask Steve.

"Sure sir, there is something that I need to clarify with you when I return, would that be in order sir?" ask Dex.

"Yes, it would be in order, I should be having a break soon and then we can talk." Says Steve

Steve knew what was on his Number one's mind he would like to know if Lydia was the spy and if there was anything between us, it is his right to know as this should not create a problem with him as he himself are in love with Janet one of his old crew members, and fellow fighter pilot, a nice girl prim and proper and always doing the right thing never do anything unless ordered to do so and then she loves him, in secret they share quarters, and I am not suppose too know that but a quick check with the computer confirmed that thought Steve.

"Lydia let us go to my quarters I would like to talk to you." says Steve.
"Sure commander I thought that you never going to ask." she said.
On the way to his quarters he first stop at the store and picked up a bottle of the best champagne
That is available on the ship; he could see that Lydia is confused, but said nothing and whistling away to his quarters.
"There we are my love, now first tell me how did that thing get into your stomach?" ask Steve friendly.
"I Do not know Steve I swear that I did not know about it, always just before my late boyfriend gets contact I had a small pain right there where it was, and it was only from that time that I got this thing, where it came from I do not know." says Lydia.

Steve could see that it is the truth; he has heard of a similar case before that they actually make you to sleep then force you to swallow it, as it is so small you remember nothing the next morning.
"I believe you, and I love you with my whole hart, from tonight onwards you are staying in this quarters and not a word to anyone, is that clear Captain?" ask Steve.
"If the commander orders so then it is so." she answers very wittingly back.

Steve gave her a long and passionate kiss and was interrupted by the computer.

"Commander I have found a match in Commander Williams ship sir, it is a flight engineer with the name Tiop employee no 122875, waiting for your orders Commander." says the computer.

"Send a message to the Admiral and a message to Commander Williams and request immediate action I suggest that they do the same we did here and use the same coordinates." says Steve.

The Admiral came on the screen two minutes later.

"Commander, thank you for your initiative, they are operating on him right now, and they will send it the same way you did but I advised them to go another five light years further to make the enemy think that we are spread out and that may hold them back a bid longer, how is you gorgeous lady doing?" ask the Admiral.

"She is doing fine sir, here she is you are welcome to talk to her you know sir." says Steve with a smile.

"Oh, hallo there captain I have good news for you, firstly upper command sent their regards and they are not going to prosecute you at all. You did what you had to do at that time and under duress as well.

Secondly a boy was delivered to headcounters early today, apparently your parents were not home so they brought your son to head quarters he is fine and in the care of Admiral Gibbs till your parents can be located." says the Admiral.

Lydia screamed and jumped into Steve's arms and kissed him on the mouth as Dex came to the open door. She is overwhelmed with joy about this news; she could not thank the Admiral enough.

The Admiral smiled he still wanted to say something to Steve but could not get a word in so he just broke contact.

"Now ,now darling calm down there is more news that might exited you but there is still work to do, I am just as glad that your son is well and save." says Steve. Steve called Dex in.

"I Am so happy now Steve you had no idea what I went through the last two months, I actually thought about taking my own life at a time till I met you, you made a difference in the way I see things now." says Lydia.

"Well I am glad it is all over now." says Steve.

"Dex, you must be wondering what is going on here?" ask Steve.

"Yes commander I actually came to you to ask you if Captain Loxton was a spy as I overheard the conversation with the Admiral." says Dex

"What I am going to tell you now Dex does not get out of this room, as it is very private and does not concern the crew at all, you may know about this as it is your right and I do trust you, is that in order with you ?" ask Steve.

Lydia was lost in her own world while they talked she was singing softly away and started cleaning Steve's room.

"Yes Commander, you know that you can trust me completely, but I do not like to keep in the dark sir." says Dex.

"I do apologies for that Dex but, there was unfortunately not enough time to talked to you as everything happened so fast, and I had to think and act very fast to avoid our fleet and our own death.." says Steve.

"Your apology is excepted Commander, if it was not for you then we were dead by now." says Dex

"Firstly that you need to know is that Captain Loxton and I are in love, this happened the moment we met and it grew all the stronger until now, are you ok on that Dex?" ask Steve.

"I Am fine on that sir, I could see the way she was looking at you the first day that I met you sir and I then knew that she admire you very much the rest of the officers also saw that sir but they will not suspect anything if you keep it low profile like you did sir." says Dex.

"Thank you Dex, now the second thing is that she was in love before with a fighter pilot and he was actually a spy, she did not know it at that time and they had a boy together, he spied for the financial gain it brings to look after them better, but when he saw through their plan he wanted out, so they knocked him off and make it looked like a normal enemy attack." says Steve

"Typical cowards." says Dex.

"They then kidnapped her son, Dunn was behind the kidnapping as well, and forced her to spy for them or she will never see her child again as they will kill him and then her too, they also manage without her knowledge to plant a tracker into her stomached that we discovered and removed, that is the package that we transported into the astral belt to fool the enemy." says Steve.

Dex thought for a moment looking at her and then to Steve.

"The Admiral and upper command are not going to prosecute her and they cleared her completely as she saved our lives to tell us what the enemy is up to the moment she learned their plans." says Steve.

"And what does the Admiral say about your relationship with her?" ask Dex.

"The Admiral is fine on that, as he said that after the war I would become an Admiral myself then this would not matter at all." says Steve.

"You getting promoted that is fantastic Commander, congratulations sir." says Dex and shook his hand.

"That is not all, Dex you yourself will take command of this ship in my place when this is all over as high commander." says Steve.

"You mean I am also getting promoted sir?" ask Dex.

"Yes Dex you are." says Steve.

"Gee. Now that is something new, I thought this is never going to happen." says Dex

"Now you can go and tell Janet this good news Dex I will excuse you now as I have other things on my mind that needs some attention." says Steve.

Dex looked at the commander surprised.

"How did you know about Janet and I sir we kept it very secret sir." says Dex.

"Not secret enough as the computer picked it up that she is staying in your quarters, besides I knew about it all along, and to me it doesn't matter as long as you can do your work I do not have a problem with that." says Steve.

"Ok then I better tell her the good news then and not a word to the others." says Dex and he was gone

Steve closed the door and took Lydia in his arms, she lay her head on his chest and hold him very stiffly.

"I Am so happy things can not get better than this, I have my son back and I have you my love, what more can a woman want?" she ask.

"There is a little something that I need to tell you that will make this even better." says Steve.

"Now what could that be?" ask Lydia

"The doctor found that you are three days pregnant with our child." says Steve.

There was a moment of silence and she looked at him with big eyes and then she held him around his neck and started to cry softly.

"What is the matter now?" ask Steve.

"I Am happy as that is what I wanted for us, I wanted to have your baby as I love you more that I loved my late husband, you are the best thing that could have happened to me." she said between the tears.

Steve opened the champagne and pours two glasses full.

"This is on your happiest day in space my dear, let us make it a lasting one." says Steve.

Steve made one last turn on the bridge and then retired for the night as they are going to reach Astoria in the morning hours due to good speed, Steve is expected to be on the bridge and he most properly will have to meet with the admiral.

Lydia and Steve made love and something was different as it was very intense and there was a feeling of melting togetherness while they made love, although Steve had to be careful as her wound was still fresh. Afterwards she fell asleep in his arms.

The phone rang and it was the bridge.

"Commander we are four light years away from Astoria, you requested us to wake you at this stage." says the bridge major.

"Thank you I will be there soon." says Steve and hang up.

Lydia was awake as well and rest her head on his shoulder. "Do you really have to get up now?" she asked.

"Very shortly my love, we can still lay for ten minutes or so." says Steve.
Her hand found what she was looking for and it was only twenty minutes
later that Steve got into the shower.

On arrival on the bridge, the major called Steve.

"Sir, there is a message from the Admiral that you must please call him
when you get on the bridge, also there is some movement in space in front
of us and we can not identify who it is yet sir." says the major.

"How far in front of us and what direction are they moving in?" ask
Steve.

"Two light years and moving in the same direction and speed as us sir."
says the major.

Steve knows that their radar can pick then up but not visually, so identification
could be difficult.

Steve decided to contact the Admiral as his equipment is far better than
what he has on this ship, the Admiral might be able to identify the ship
that is moving in front of us.

'" Admiral good morning, did you sleep well sir?" ask Steve

"Good morning Steve, no actually I did not sleep yet as I was busy
organizing war strategy with the generals the whole time up to now, and
you Steve how was your evening?" Ask the Admiral.

"Wonderful Admiral she is very good for me, there is a ship in front of us
sir, and we cannot identify it, is it possible that you can see who it is as
we are not aware of anyone over taking us, it could also be the enemy
that left before us and got trough somewhere else, and are now in front
of us?" ask Steve.

"Let us have a look, Yes I can see them, it is three Slikton mother ships in single file, they will reach Austria in one and a half hours, our fighters would reach them in twenty minutes." says the Admiral.

"We will be ready to leave in fifteen minutes sir, as I will need to brief our pilots first as we do not know if their shields were affected or not sir." says Steve.

"That is fine I will also sent some of our fighters to join up with you as soon as you leave and good luck commander." says the Admiral

"RED ALERT" Flashed lights all over the ship and an alarm screams everybody awake, Steve spoke into an intercom.

"All fighter pilots to the boardroom all other personnel to battle stations." says Steve.

On the ships monitor he could see how people run in all different directions, and he saw how Lydia run down to the boardroom still buttoning up her blouse.

"Computer has all the fighters including this vessel been loaded with microchips?" ask Steve

"Yes commander, all they have to do is to fire an the enemy and their shields will corrupt immediately, I have also made it contagious so that the virus could spread to other ships and I have made it a changeable virus as they introduce anti virus so it will take up another form and we are immune to this virus sir." answer the computer.

"Thank you computer." says Steve and went to the board room.

When he got there he looked at the pilots still trying to get dressed, Dex sits there still fast asleep and Janet is trying to come her hear, Lydia looks perfect and gave him quite a nice smile. Then Steve got hold of the Admiral. The Admiral's face came on the screen, and a stir went trough the pilots as they know from experience that if the Admiral is with them in a meeting then it is serious stuff. Dex rather woke up when he saw the Admiral on the screen.

"Admiral it looks like all the pilots are here now, how many crafts can you sent with us sir?" ask Steve.

"Fifteen should be enough don't you think Steve?" ask the Admiral.

"Can you make it sixteen sir?" ask Steve.

"Sure sixteen it is." says the Admiral.

"Ladies and gentleman, we have a situation here that three Slikton mother ships are two light years in front of us and will reach Astoria before us, therefore it is our responsibility to stop them and wipe them out of space, there is no place for them here, not so close to home anyway. "Says Steve.

"Now, your shields has been upgraded to withstand their rockets, and we have given them a virus that will corrupt their shields, so that our weapons can be effective against them as they created a sound barrier in their shields, that is why we are retreating to Astoria to defend the planet, and to give us more time to figure this out. You have rockets loaded on your crafts if everything fails then use them." says Steve.

"Any questions?" Ask Steve.

"The competition sir can it start now?" ask one of the pilots.

Steve looked at the Admiral and the Admiral started to smile very wide

"Yes sure why not." says the Admiral and the pilots cheer so loudly that Steve could not get a word in, so he pluck the headphones in to hear what the Admiral was saying.

"What competition is that now Steve?" ask the Admiral.

"That is the pilot who has the most kills can take his wife and children or if not married his father and mother and girlfriend to any location in the galaxy for a month holiday on the fleet's account sir and that competition is open for the whole fleet sir." says Steve.

"Wow, that is a tough one, ok let us do it, I will put it in writing to the whole fleet and take whatever upper command through at me or in this case us." says the Admiral.

Steve had to silence the pilots.

"We are going to attack in two waves; the first wave is going to be let by Major Kick and his squadron and with eight of the Admirals crafts. Directly behind them is the rest to follow in two intermitted waves. Let by Dex and the remainder of the Admirals crew, I will need five pilots here to protect the ship incase we need to defend it. Any volunteers?" ask Steve.

No one put there hands up. slowly Captain Loxton put her hand up, then Janet and two of the other woman pilots, that made it four, but Steve except that as he himself will also go out if they are attacked.

"Now the first wave go in from the back with high speed and shoot bluntly at the rear mother ship, then the next one, and then the front one. Your purpose is not so much to kill the ship but to corrupt the shields, then you go around hard but wide. The second split wave is then hitting hard the rear ship and all the other ships in line, the split rear then hits anything hard that still moves. The first wave then came again, and if the mother ships still exist, then you hit it hard with rockets, and then the second split wave also with rockets and what ever you have. Said Steve.

"Any questions?" ask Steve.

"None, right move out and good luck I would like to see you all here again afterwards and I mean all of you." says Steve

The Admiral gave thumps up in approval for Steve's plan; he knows that when Steve works something out it works no matter what.

"Ladies to the bridge and I will take coffee as well." says Steve
The woman pilots laugh and the race was on to be the first on the bridge
with coffee for the Commander.

On the bridge there the ladies were each with two cups of coffee in their
hands one for themselves and one for Steve, Steve were careful not to
heard feelings so he said.
"I Will drink all of them thank you very much that was very kind of you
all." says Steve.

Together they watch as the first wave hit the ships, Steve could see clearly
how the shields go green in color as it corrupted, then another shield
formed but also corrupted, then the next wave hit the ships and Steve could
see how the ships started to fall apart, some fighters escaped specially
from the front ship. Then the split wave arrived and fighters disintegrated
in mid space. Then Major Kick and his first wave came in again and took
on what was left. A few rockets was fired on to the front ship as it was still
mostly intact, and it also exploded.
"Mission complete enemy destroyed. "says Dex over the radio.
"Roger, do a three sixty and return to base, and well done." says Steve
over the radio.
The Admiral came on the screen.
"That was good, I must admit that I was unsure if we are going to get
past their shields but you have done it Steve congratulations." says the
Admiral.

"You have to thank the onboard computer for that plan sir I only asked and
it came up with the solution all by it self sir." says Steve

"That was brilliant of you to think of that, in any case that is what the computer is there for." says the Admiral and rang off.

The first of the pilots arrive home and you could clearly hear on the racket they are making that the moral is very high now. "Steve thought to himself, that this was exactly what the pilots needed right now to show that they can do the job and that every thing is not lost after all."
Steve smiled very wide as he entered the boardroom.
"That was one hell of a nice attack I am sure you all enjoyed the kills that you have made, let us see, for who was this there first real contact within the enemy?" ask Steve.

Many hands jumped in the air.
"Good, who of you lot did not get a kill?" ask Steve.
One hand went up in the air, it was a young officer that only just came out of training and Steve knew that he need to boost this pilot as they are the bravest and can fold into apathy fast if not boosted to top performance.
"What did you shoot at so that you can say that you do not have a kill?" ask Steve friendly.
"I was shooting at the mother ships sir." says the pilot.
"Computer, show us the video of this airman's craft and confirm kills?" ask Steve.
The video started to play at the first run and you see how the pilot brings his craft directly over the mother ships and fire away with the correct song. You see how the shields cave in and how the new shields form and cave in again, then you see the pilot scooting at the hard of the mother ship and actually hit it, causing it to explode the engineering.
Then you see the same thing happening over the second mother ship and the third mother ship, when they came over for the second time you can see that there is nothing left and how the pilot seek a target, when he came

to the front mother ship it has not completely died yet so you can see how the pilot released four rockets into the mother ship killing it completely.

"Airman what is your name, stand on your chair and then tell me your name?" ask Steve

The pilot got up on his chair and very red-faced said.

"My name is Airman Darral Poke sir."

"Now Darrel, you know that if you shoot a person on the ground then it gives you one point, if you shoot a craft that will be two points, but if you shoot a mother ship and killed it then you get awarded ten points, did you know that Darral ?" ask Steve.

"No sir, I did not know it." says the Airman Darral.

"W ell you just got yourself thirty points there and I am sure that everyone in this room agree with me that this was accurate shooting from your side and you actually did kill them all, so Darral you have three mother ship kills behind you mate." says Steve and started to clap hands for this brave young man.

The rest of the crew did not wait and cheered this poor airman so that Steve could not get a word in. "Now that is high moral, "thought Steve as he left the boardroom as he knows that he would not get another word in. Dex saw him leave and gave him the thump up sigh, he will carry on with the meeting, and Steve went to his quarters and phone the entertainment officer.

"you can expect some very loud pilots coming your way, nothing stronger than beer as they still might need to fly again today but I will try and avoid that." says Steve.

"That is in order sir, Commander Dex did phone me just now to say that a whole lot of you are coming, as they had a very good fight and won it." says the officer.

"Right, I am sure that you will hear every detail of it, and many times as well." says Steve and rang off.

Steve dialed, and the Admiral's face appeared on the screen, smiling from ear to ear.

"You know Steve this is the first time in this war that we have had kills without casualties from our side, and that is only because you sheared your information with us, and in such a way upgraded the fleet, the rest of the fleet is now so exited as they saw on video what our pilots have done and they cant wait to get in on the action. The Asteroid pilots are all in the pub trying there best to lift the roof I had to escape to my office." says the Admiral.

"It is the same here sir, is it possible that Captain Loxton and one of our other pilots can go to Astoria as soon as we are in position? As I feel that she must go and see her son, the other pilot do have a very sick mom and I have confirmation on that sir, she is most properly not going to make the night." says Steve.

"Steve I would suggest that you take them there yourself as this is a war situation and I will feel more comfortable to have you with them, but only for the night, I will take over your ship if need be, I will actually look forward to that, but Steve go and meet the parents and if anything comes up I will call you on your personal communicator just have it on you." says the Admiral.

"Thank you sir we will leave as soon as we are in position." says Steve and broke connection before the Admiral changes his mind, not that he ever does but just in case.

Steve went to the bridge; there he sent an orderly to the pub with a message for flight lieutenant Pine and Captain Loxton to meet him on the bridge immediately.

Steve started to scan space where they are going to camp and there is no sign of the enemy for five light years around the planet as Steve can see the whole planet from where he sits. Lydia and Pine came running to him they salute and entered the bridge. Pine is a man in his early thirties and is apparently a very good shot with a handgun, and by the looks of him also with the woman.

However, Steve is not worried as Lydia will not go down rank on herself, besides she has him the highest rank on this ship, to fall for any other rank would be foolish.

"Come in, Captain I have received orders to take you to your parents and to drop Pine of at his mothers place, but it is only for tonight, tomorrow morning at seven we must leave to be back here by seven thirty, as there is a war on and we can not take special leave at this stage, also nothing gets told to anyone on the planet, we do not want a scare on the planet is that clear. You just came through and is leaving in the morning again, that is It." says Steve.

Lydia stands there with a big smile on her face and Steve knows what she is thinking, a real mother.

"We will be in position in ten minutes and I want you to get your stuff and meet me at my ship in ten minutes sharply.," says Steve.

The Admiral took over command as they took up their position. Steve spoke to Dex very briefly and he nodded his head in approval that Lydia must see her kid that is very important

Steve could not speak as per say to Dex as the pub was so full that over a distance he just gave sign language with face expressions and he is sure that Dex got the message, to be sure Steve write him a memo saying took Capt Loxton to see her child be back in morning, Admiral is in charge he will call you if necessary enjoy your evening.

Steve arrives at his ship late and found two irritated pilots standing there waiting for him, "sharply he said." says Lydia in a mockery type of voice, but with a smile.

"I tell you what, I will buy you and your son a mc Donald's for that, last orders you know.," says Steve as he started to do a preflight.

"Pre flight is already done sir.," says Lydia.

"Thank you and are there twenty rockets on board?" ask Steve.

"I don't know, did not check for that sir.," says Lydia firmly

Steve checked and then when he was satisfied lift of for the planet. Once he was outside the mother ship, he opened, his ships speed valves and they traveled twice the speed of light and exhilarating x10 % per second due to gravity pull.

"This is dangerous to fly so fast to a planet sir.," warned Lydia.

"Yes I do know that very well, I lost two crew members in such an accident before, but in this case it is necessary as we do not want the enemy to get a lock on us as they then can see where we land." says Steve.

"Now, that makes sense, if I would have come on my own I would have flown slowly to my parent's house and would not even thought of this., "says Lydia.

At that moment they started to hit the atmosphere of the planet and Steve immediately pulled up at an angle to avoid them breaking up and then as soon a the impact was gone pushed the craft down to the surface, within a few seconds they were flying at low level with the planet and lined up on the hospital were his mom was lying dying.

"Now, that is flying.," says Lydia.

"Only an expert can fly like that, and it was a super experience commander.," says pine.

Then suddenly the craft shut down and went into limp mode, Steve tries to get it back but was not able to "computer, what is going on? "ask Steve.

"That is the air traffic police that disabled the craft. "

The traffic police landed next to the craft and Steve were ordered to get out

Steve got out of the craft and was furious with the police. "I am high commander Steve Holt; you do not have the authority to disable any military crafts." Said Steve.

"I am sorry commander, but we do have all the authority to do so to any craft military or the not. You flew at a speed far exceeding the maximum allowed speed, and are now under arrest. Said the officer.

"You can not do that." Said Steve.

"And why not commander, why did you fly so fast?" ask the officer.

"I am on a mission that is sensitive of nature and I think that it is better to speak to the admiral yourself." said Steve

"We will do that." Said the officer.

Steve page through to the admiral and after a short conversation to the admiral called the officer into the craft.

The officer could not keep his eyes of Lydia when he saw her. The admiral explained to the officer that the mission the commander is on is top secret and by keeping him there is jeopardizing the security of the fleet and that he must released the commander immediately.

"Admiral I understand that the commander is on a mission but he must not fly so fast as that is putting other crafts at risk." Said the officer.

"It is important for the commander to move at the speed he is doing in order to avoid being traced down by our enemy spies as they can not track him if he travels fast. He is ordered by me to do so and I have more authority than your chief of staff. So beat it and let the commander go." said the Admiral

The officer then enables the craft and after a long look at Lydia said goodbye and left.

"We might have to use these officers in the near time to come, if it wasn't for that I would have liked to feed that man's tactical to the dogs." Said Steve as he lifts off.

Lydia grinned from ear to ear and said "sis on you commander the poor officer did not expect to see a nice looking girl here.

"That is true." Says Pine

"Computer can you prevent the police from disabling us?" ask Steve

"That has been done already commander." Says the computer

"Good feed that through to all our ships, and I would like to get that technology to be able to use it on our enemy's ships'" says Steve

"I will work on that commander." Says the computer.

"Very clever commander." Said Lydia with a few Yeah year's from Pine

Steve landed on the roof of the hospital and noticed that the police craft is following him at a distance. "Computer can you use their system on them and disable that craft?" ask Steve

"Yes commander I can." Says the computer

"Then do it now." Says the commander.

"It is done sir." Said the computer

"Let the fun begin." Says Steve as they watched the police craft landing on the grass outside the hospital, and a very confused officer stepping out of his craft looking directly at them as they lift of from the hospital.

Steve and Lydia see him of and left for her parent's house.

Once again Steve opened up the ship's valves and within seconds they were flying supersonic and he had to hold the ship back not to go to fast as it will cause damage to the planet's surface and that will not be the best move as the enemy then has a way to track them down.

Her parent's home was on the horizon when he suddenly change direction and flew away from the house but in such a way that the house could be seen. Steve scans the house to see if there is anything out of place but can't see inside the house. "Computer, scan the house and surrounding areas, I need to know how many people are in the house." Ask Steve.

"There are 3 persons in the house, two adults and a child. "Says the computer.

Steve could see the excitement in Lydia's face.

Steve landed the craft, and before he could shut it down Lydia was out of the door running up to the house, bursting in the front door, he could hear her scream with delight as she swept her boy off his feet and held him close to her chest. Tears of joy ran down her cheeks as she spoke softly to her son.

Steve did not get out of the craft. "Computer. Scan the people and the house for any tractor beams or listening devices."

"There is a listening device under the lamb in the lounge and one in the main bedroom under the dressing table, there is also a tractor beam in the boy's stomach." Say's the computer.

Steve got out of the craft and as he went in to the house he showed to her parents to be quiet, he then went ahead and collected the listening devices and destroyed them.

.

Steve instantly recognize her dad, he was working as an engineer on a scientific ship that collected plants from other planets in order to produce food. Steve was at that time as Alison a junior captain on the same ship before he got promoted and went to a battle ship.

After the greetings her dad asked Steve what did he do going through the house. Steve explained that listening devices were placed into the house and he had to destroy them.

Lydia was lost in the arms of her son and did not even hear the conversation between her dad and him, Lydia looked a lot like her mother, a very attractive woman in her late sixties, but she look no older than forty, and he wondered what her secret was and if Lydia is going to look as good as her mom at that age. That is if they are going to make it through the war coming, that grim thought hit him hard and he did not expect the emotion that got hold of him at that moment, he did not even hear what her dad was saying.

At that moment the buzzer went of on his belt, Lydia looked up and Steve could see the stress on her face and he knows that she knows that that could only be the admiral. Steve excused himself and disappeared into the craft to contact the admiral.

When Steve got out there was a sense of urgency in his attitude and he went to Lydia and softly told her they need to get to the mother ship urgently something has happen that needs his urgent attention.
"Commander please tells me what is going on, is there a war coming?" asks her dad.

"Sir what I am going to tell you is top secret and for the time being please not a word to anyone, is that understood sir?" said Steve
"Yes commander not a word from me." Said her dad.

"First of all sir, you need to take her child to the local hospital as there is a tracking device placed in his stomach, and it needs to be removed and then destroyed, is that understood sir." Asked Steve,
"Yes commander that is clearly understood." Said her father.

"There is a war coming, and we are all at risk, the enemy is planning to attack the planet in order to mine it for they're purpose, there will be no survivors if we allow them to come through, that is the reason that we are here." Explain Steve

"I Understand commander, now that I know what is going to happen, I will keep this to myself." Said her dad.

Steve took Lidia by her hand and they say goodbye to her parents and she gave her son a huge hug, then they got into the craft and lift off with great speed.

"What did the Admiral want?" asks Lidia

"One of our mother ships was attacked and we suffered losses, our weapons had no effect on them." Said Steve.

"That is horrible." Said Lydia as they docked in the mother ship.

Steve found Dex on the bridge. "What happened?" asked Steve.

Dex took out a disc, "I have a full report for you sir" said Dex
"Let us look at it in the board room" said Steve

Dex activate the computer and what Steve saw gave him the horrors

They were looking from the eye view of the mother ship that was hit, two ships of the sliktons were coming to into view and the computer recognized them as friends and not as enemy, Steve remembered the order he gave to the hole fleet that they are not friends and that the computer has to be programmed that way.

They saw how the sliktons fire a stream of rockets to the ship, the first five hit and collapsed the shields and then the rest of the rockets hit the ship with full destructive force. The mid section of the ship was completely destroyed and the ship was burning uncontrollably.

The commander then ordered high alert and then called for help as the section that was hit was the docking stations of the ship and no fighters could scramble.

The mother ship then returned fire, but the wrong song was played and had no effect.

At that moment two of Steve's ship's crafts came into view as they were on a sortie in the area, and they attacked the sliktons and destroyed them in an instant.

.

"What happened to the ship?" asked Steve.
"The ship was evacuated and a repair ship was sent to the ship to see what they could do, there is eighty crew dead and one hundred and sixty crew wounded most of them with burn wounds, Sir" answered Dex.

Steve looked down at the table for a moment and then said "that was the first casualty of war, and it happened because orders were not followed and inadequate training".

"You are correct sir." Said Dex

"Please excuse me for a while I am going to see the admiral, and give this order to the hole fleet." Said Steve
Steve writes an order that once again the sliktons are enemy and then he gave the correct song to destroy the sliktons.
"Yes sir I do that right now." Said Dex

Steve found the Admiral in front of his computer in his quarters

"Hi commander please come in and have a seat." Says the Admiral
"Thank you sir" said Steve as he sits next to the Admiral
The Admiral was studying the attack and just shook his head.
What do you think of that?" asked the Admiral
"The commander disobeyed my direct order sir and the gunman played the wrong song sir" said Steve

"That is a disgrace, I already got that commander on orders to have a court marshal, and he should be punished for this incident, so that it can not happen again." Said the Admiral.

"That is fine sir, but do not be too hard on the commander sir as we need him and his crew in the upcoming battle sir." Said Steve

"I hear what you are saying Steve, but I have to be hard so that the fleet can see that we take our command seriously and that weakness of this sort would not be tolerated," bark the Admiral

Steve knew better as to argue with the Admiral

"The injured crew has been taken to the surface for treatment at their hospitals as we do not want to deplete our supplies in space. Said the Admiral.

"Now the whole planet is going to know that we are at war sir." Said Steve

"I gave the order that it was a space accident, but we can not linger any longer, we have to alert the defense force of the treat and upgrade their weapon system and train them at the same time. "Said the Admiral

At that moment the memo Steve has written came up on the Admiral's screen.

"excellent commander, that is what is going to make us win this war, with you in charge of the fleet, the enemy has no change of winning this war, that is why I am sending you back to your ship right now so that you can take over from me while I handle the defense force on the planet. "Said the Admiral.

"How do you mean in charge of the fleet, sir? "Asks Steve

"I have written a memo that you are the commanding officer in control of this war and that all commanders have to report to you and you only, and to follow your orders to the point. You see Steve you are the next generation Admiral and that is already in writing from fleet command, but to make sure that all these generals and political screw ups don't bug you while this war is going on, your promotion will only come to effect after the war." Explain the Admiral.

Steve was silent for a moment while the information sinks in, this is a big step forward and he was dreaming for this moment.
"Thank you Admiral." Says Steve that was all he could think of to say at that moment.
"You will report to me and me alone concerning this war." Says the Admiral
"Yes sir." Answer Steve
"Now get back to your ship and win this war fast and with minimum losses to us." Ordered the Admiral.
With a salute Steve departed.

Steve arrives on the bridge of his ship feeling emotionally drained but he knows that it is not the time to be weak.
"Dex sent an order for all ship commanders to report to the board room of our ship in five hours time, for a brief meeting, and get all our officers in the board room immediately." asks Steve.
"Yes Sir." Replied Dex

Steve could see that he received the Admiral's memo and he could sense the respect from the man.
Steve went to his quarters and took a shower and dress in battle dress.

An orderly clerk softly knocks on his door and informed him that all the officers are waiting for him in the board room as he has requested.

.Steve was greeted by a very silent board room as he entered. "Commander on the deck." Shouted Dex as he entered.
All the officers jumped up and saluted him.
"Please be seated." Says Steve
"now as you all know the Admiral placed me in charge of the war and of the fleet during this war, therefore I can not command this ship any longer as I am going to be very busy planning and so on." Says Steve

A stir went though the officers and he saw Lydia staring at him, and he knew that that must be a shock for her and the other officers.
"Therefore it has become time to hand over the ships command over to Dex as the commander of this vessel and major Kick as second in charge and that is in effect immediately." Said Steve

Clapping of hands and cheering for the new command is taking over the board room.
Dex jump up and quiet every one down
"Thank you sir, but what rank does you have then now sir and are you leaving us?" Ask Dex.

"I will still be the rank of commander and are not leaving you at all, I will only move to other quarters to make space for you, but you run this ship from now on Dex.." says Steve.

"Lydia would you please help me to clean my quarters and help me to redecorate my new quarters." Asked Steve
"It would be a pleasure sir" she answer sweetly

Lydia and Steve left the very noisy board room and when they were alone she kissed him softly and just held him in her arms.

"Are you moving in with me?" she asks

"I wish I could, but no I have selected quarters next to yours so that we could choose where to sleep for the duration of this war." He replied

Steve took up the inter ship communicator and dialed the mess.

"There is 360 commanders coming to the ship for a meeting, please prepare snacks and drinks and prepare the big boardroom for the meeting." Order Steve

After listening for a moment he replied "three hours from now." And rang off

Lydia and Steve packed up his quarters and redecorated his new quarters next to Lydia's and Steve was surprised by the way Lydia move his personal belongings in such a way only a woman could, she took a cloth from her quarters and made a table cloth out of it and placed his computer on top of it. He never thought that it would look as good as what it did.

Then it was time for the big meeting. Steve arrived at the boardroom full of commanders with the same rank as what he has, some of them are in the service much longer than he is and in a way he felt inferior to them but dismissed that thought and said to himself that they did nothing for the fleet but to follow orders, and that is what they need to do now as well.

"High commander on the deck." Shouted Dex

Every commander jump up on attention. Those made Steve blush a bit as he did not expect it, as they all have the same rank.

"As you were thank you Dex." Said Steve

"Now as you all know the Admiral has placed me in charge of the war, but I can not do it alone, I do need each and every one of you to help the fleet to win this war." Said Steve.

A few yes that is true was heard

"I want all of you to come up with practical advice of how we are going to protect Astoria from the enemy, but not right now do it over a period of two days and let me know, what is important is to train your crew on the weapon system as much as possible so that what happened to that other mother ship do not happen again." Said Steve

"I suggest that we do small sorties in an area and practice the system." Said one of the commanders.

"That is a good idea, but do a lot of simulation drills with the crew in order for each crew member to know what he or she must do and when." Said Steve

"What are our chances to win this war?" ask another commander

"If we do exactly what we were trained for and we follow exact orders , then we stand a good chance to win, but it might be a lengthy war with casualties on both sides." Said Steve.

"What are the plans for the war?" ask another commander

"As of now the Admiral and I are working on certain strategies to fight the enemy, and we will let you know, as for this moment I want you to stay in position and do not let any enemy ship goes pass you." Said Steve

"Well enjoy the snacks and return to your ships as soon as possible and wait for further orders." Said Steve and left the board room.

Steve felt tired and drained after the meeting and went to his quarters and went to sleep a bit.

Then his buzzer woke him

"Commander, did you have a good rest?" ask the Admiral.

"Yes sir I needed it badly." Said Steve

"Good, now the sliktons were spotted by our cameras fifteen light years from here and are holding their position in that area, I am surprised that they got through the astral belt so soon." Said the Admiral

"So am I Admiral, I will investigate that immediately sir." Said Steve

"Good report back to me what ever you found, I think the war is about to start." Said the Admiral. And logged off.

Lydia woke up during the conversation and looked scared up to Steve.

"Do not be concerned my love, it is only the beginning of the end one way or the other." Said Steve

"Don't tell me that, I am very scared at this moment." Said Lydia

"I would like to hold you in comfort but I can't right now as my real work has started and I need to go now." Said Steve.

She kissed him softly and he runs out the door to the bridge.

Steve found Dex on the bridge.

"Commander on the deck." Shouted Dex

"Thank you Dex, please do a 360 on the star map 15 light years from here I need to see what is going on there." Asks Steve

The star map lit up and the surge began, they saw the silkons build up in the west and then they also saw another build up of enemy ships to the north but much closer than the sliktons.

"I wonder what the are up to." Said Dex

"They are planning to surround us." Said Steve

"What do you suggest we do sir?" Ask Dex

"Look at the east and the south, and you will see movement of enemy ships in the area, they are waiting for orders to assemble at a certain point, what we need to do is to guess where that is going to be and then spoil that for them." Said Steve

"How are we going to spoil that for them Sir? Ask Dex

"We are going to place space mines in the area." Said Steve
"What is that sir, I have never heard of such a thing before?" ask Dex
"I know, I just thought of a thing like that, I will design and build one right now. "Said Steve
"How is it going to work Sir?" ask Dex very curiously

"It is basically a rock fitted with our weapon system that is programmed with our enemy craft details and with what song to ply when it fires, so as soon as a ship is in range it will fire automatically and destroy the target, I will also program it so that we can de- activate or activate it from our command centre with a self destruct mechanism should it be captured and in the event that we do not need it anymore. "Explain Steve.

"That sounds like you have got that all worked out Sir" said Dex
"I am in engineering if you need me, seeing the possible locations that you think they are going to use then call Me." said Steve
"Will do so sir." Said Dex
.

Steve worked with engineering and he could sense the respect the engineers have for him, they love his idea and are working with enthusiasm to complete the task

Then they were ready for testing the mine, but there were nothing at this moment to test it on and Steve ordered them to manufacture a couple of thousand of these mines.

Material for the mines will be order from the planet and coming from engineering no suspicion should be created as security is of the outmost importance. Steve ordered that one of the completed mines be placed into the cargo hold for transportation.

Then Steve contacted the Admiral

"Admiral I came up with a device that should be the solution to our problems, I am sending the drawings and the product to you it needs to be tested." Said Steve

"I am glad you came up with something, I actually were waiting to see what you are going to come up with." said the Admiral.

Steve sends the information to the admiral and then transfers the mine to the asteroid

A soft knock on his door, Steve stood up and then suddenly the computer locked all the doors of the cabin and installed a force field locking the visitor to the wall.

Security was alerted the same time. Steve was caught by surprise and asks the computer.

"Computer explains why you took action and identify the person." Said Steve

"The intruder is a visitor from another ship sir, and he came to you with a weapon in his hand, his intention to you was not friendly but hostile." Said the computer

"Security is here sir you may come out now it is safe." Said the computer

Steve knows that the computer is programmed to protect the commanders at all times also in the case of mutiny.

Steve went out of the door to find Mr. Dunn standing there glaring at him and Steve could see the hate in the man's eyes.

"Take him away and lock him up and guard him till I can find out what to do with him." Ordered Steve.

Cold shiver s went through Steve as a thought struck his mind, Lydia I must check on her.

Steve knocks on her door but there was no answer so he ran back to his quarters and asks the computer.

"Computer locates Lydia."

"Lydia is in the mess with the rest of the crew having something to eat sir." Said the computer.

He could not believe the relief he was experiencing, he contact the Admiral.

"Admiral we have a security leak somewhere, the computer pinned Dunn to the wall at my new quarters with a weapon in his hand, he wanted to kill me. We arrested him and are waiting for orders from you Sir." Said Steve.

"The computer informed me of the incident as it was programmed to do, as you know all commanders in the fleet are to be protected and incidence like this one gets reported immediately, sent Dunn over to me we will deal with him here, I am aware of the leak and our intelligent section will find the source from Dunn." Said the Admiral

"I will do so sir, do you think that this has anything to do with the mines I created?" ask Steve.

"No I do not think so, I think it is because you are in charge of the war, the mines you created will be tested in one hour's time, we located an lonely enemy craft and transferred the mine in its path, it should reach it in one hour, if you would like to see what happens then come over soon and then we watch it together. "Said the Admiral

"I will be delighted sir." Said Steve

Steve contacted security and asked them to bring Dunn to transport bay no 5 he then went to transport bay 5 and waited a moment for them, Dunn gave security a rough time when he saw where they were taking him, but they did not take his nonsense. Steve transferred Dunn to the asteroid.

Lydia came to meet him at the transport bay shortly after he transferred Dunn.

"My love are you ok? I have just heard what happened." Said Lydia

"I am ok, the enemy has got a price on my head as I am in charge of the war and they are scared." said Steve

"Silly bastards." Said Lydia

"Are you joining me on the bridge?" ask Steve

"It would be my pleasure, you need somebody close to you to look after you at all times." said Lydia

"Dex did you manage to locate possible locations?" ask Steve

"Yes sir, there are three possibilities, let me show you sir." Said Dex

Dex lit up the star map and circled the three areas he identified.

"Good I think that you are right, let me sent this to the Admiral I do have a meeting with him, and Dex nobody leaves or enters this vessel without your authority from this moment on." Said Steve

"That is in order sir we have heard of the incident and I am busy finding out how he got on board sir." Said Dex

"That would be good to know and also were he came from." Said Steve

"It is time for me to go to the Admiral, keep me informed at all times." Said Steve

"Will do that sir." said Dex

"Can I come with you?" ask Lidia

"Not at this time my love, but do get some rest there is not going to be time for rest in the near time to come." Said Steve

"Ok but come to me when you return." She asks

"I can't wait for that." Said Steve. While he gave her a hug

Steve transported himself to the asteroid and went to the Admiral; the Admiral was in conversation with security when Steve arrived.

"Steve good you are here, Dunn broke loose and started running so security shot him, he is dead." Said the Admiral

"Pity we would like to know who sent him, Dex is finding out where he came from at this moment." Said Steve

"It is a shame that he is dead but also a blessing as he was creating a lot of problems for the fleet." said the Admiral as they walked into onto the bridge.

"The enemy ship is within range and we are going to activate the mine now. Let us see if this is going to work Steve." Said the Admiral

"I can not see how it is not going to work sir." Said Steve

The engineer press the arming button and the mine is armed, Steve could see the ship coming and worked out that the ship is going to pass one hundred meters from the mine which in turn would be deadly for the ship.

As the ship reach the mine the mine fired, the first shot is the shield virus that collapse the shields of the ship, then three more shots were fired and they were direct hits, she ship shook and started burning, then the ship returned fire but the mine held its position as the shields of the mine held. The mine fired again three shots and the ship was completely destroyed

Every one on the bridge was shouting and clapping hands, the Admiral was smiling from ear to ear tapping Steve on the shoulders.
"Well done commander you have exceeded yourself once again, and you are going to save a lot of lives through these mines. I want them build and placed at ten and five light years around the planet, starting with the new coordinates you sent me and once again thank you for doing this." Said the Admiral.

"That is what I am here for sir." Said Steve
"How many mines are ready to deploy at this moment?" ask the Admiral
"I am not sure sir, but I am on my way back to my ship and will let you know sir." Said Steve.
"You can just send me a memo, as I am going into a meeting with the boring generals, at leased I have some good news to tell them." Said the Admiral

At that moment the buzzer on Steve's belt went mad, he read what is written to him and without a word gave it to the admiral to read, Dunn came from the coordinates of the asteroid the Admiral is on.
"I think we must keep the information of the mines a secret a bit longer sir." Said Steve
The Admiral got a bit white in the face with this new information in his hand, he suddenly realized that he can not even trust his own crew, and questions like where did Dunn came from and how did he transported to Steve's ship without any one noticing.
"I agree commander, I will also investigate my own crew, and It looks like we have a spy on board of the asteroid." Said the Admiral.

"I will leave you to that sir, and I can only hope that we find that spy fast." Said Steve

"We must do so quickly, you must get to your ship now as there was an attempt on your live already, I do not want you to stay in the open for to long, you are to valuable for me and the fleet." Said the Admiral

"I am leaving now sir, and do not worry about me, I can take care of myself, I am just as concerned about you sir. Said Steve as he was leaving the Admiral

Steve arrived on the bridge and found major kick in command.

"Good day major how is the development in the east of here?" ask Steve

"Good day commander, there has been a little build up of ships, but they all moved out in different directions sir, just to assemble again at another location which is strange." Said Kick

"Ok just keep on monitoring it, I have a feeling that they are doing this on purpose to draw our attention away from the main force that is getting in position right now." Said Steve.

"Do you know where they are building up sir?" ask Kick

"I do not know for sure, but it will be out of our range of vision, I can assure you of that. I am going to engineering if you need me." Said Steve.

At engineering Steve establish that two thousand mines are ready for employment.

"Take five hundred to cargo bay two and one thousand to cargo bay one." Ordered Steve.

Then Steve went to his quarters to freshen up and get something to eat, just to find lydia fast asleep on his bed.

He softly kissed her and she woke up.

"Where have you been, I have been worried sick about you?" she asks

"I have been with the Admiral for a while and can not stay long as I have a lot of things to do still in a very short space of time." Said Steve.

"I miss you." Said Lydia

"Miss you to, but you will have to get used to the fact that I am very busy right now, and that does not mean that I do not love you any more, in fact I love you more and more by the moment." Said Steve

"That makes me feel much better, are you staying for a while?" ask Lydia

"No I just want to eat something small then I am off again." said Steve

"Ok I will order some food while you rest." said Lydia

"Steve ate quietly next to Lydia, wondering what the outcome of the war is going to be, as they are fighting a very capable nation with technology that they do not have yet, and that thought scared him.

Then as he finished his meal his buzzer went off, it was engineering telling him that the mines are ready.

"I have to go now my love." Said Steve

"I know my love; I will be waiting for you." Said Lydia

Steve went to cargo bay two and contacted the bridge.

"Major Kick where are the build up now?" ask Steve

"The build up has reached six hundred ships sir, the biggest yet, there coordinates are 12, 05 west and 34, 03 south sir." Said Kick

"Thank you major." Said Steve and rang off.

Steve lit the star map and found the location on the map, he saw more ships approaching and he new then where to place the mines.

First thing Steve did was to arm all the mines as where he is placing them is within shot distance from all the ships. Than he programmed the location of the mines as each mine has a serial number, it makes it easy to arm or disarm the mine and you could also move the mine to another location as need it.

Steve sent the mines off and watch with excitement how the mines as they arrive at their location they immediately lock on and fire on the ships, destroying every ship in its path. Within seconds all enemy ships has been destroyed and Steve programmed the mines again to another location right in the way of the other approaching ships.

Then Steve went to cargo hold one and armed the mines, he then programmed the mines ten light years away around the planet and sent them off.

His buzzer went mad on his side from the bridge and from the admiral, but he ignored all of that till he was finished with the sending of the mines. He also placed two mines between the debris of the ships that has been destroyed just incase enemy ships get there from another direction.

Then he went to the bridge
"Commander something weird has happened, something fired on the enemy and they all got destroyed, I do not understand it sir." Said Kick. Dex also searches the star map to see if he could spot anything that could have done it.
"I know what did it, I placed some mines in the middle of the fleet of enemy ships and as soon as they were destroyed moved them to another location, so that they could not be detected by our enemies but left two on the scene to shoot other curious ships if they come to near." Said Steve

"Mines I don't understand sir, what is that?" ask Kick

Dex was at that moment smiling from ear to ear.

"Dex will explain to you how that works, Dex here is the serial numbers of all the mines active in the area, you can move them around as you please with our transporter units, you are from now on in charge of moving and deploying the mines. Contact engineering for all the remainder of mines and placed them around the planet five years away of the planet, you will see that I have already covered ten mile radius and they are all armed.

Here are all the details of how to operate them, study them and use them well while we can. This is our first line of defense against the enemy." Explain Steve

"That is brilliant sir, I will study this immediately." Said Dex

"I am going to see the Admiral he can't stop buzzing me." Said Steve

"I don't blame him sir." Said Dex

Steve just smiled and left for the Admiral.

Steve found the Admiral in the board room full of war generals, the generals were looking baffled and were arguing about what could be the cause of this new (threat) they are facing. The Admiral excused himself from them when he saw Steve.

"I can not congratulate you enough for the success of the mines Steve, you did a great job." Said the Admiral.

"Thank you sir I was just doing what was expected of me." Said Steve

"Don't be so modest my friend, tell me how did you make the mines disappear so fast after the attack and then reappear two of them again minutes later." ask the Admiral

"I did make some small changes to the program sir we could move them to other locations using our transporter unit sir." said Steve

"That is brilliant Steve, what do I tell these monkeys in the board room?" ask the Admiral.

"Sir I think it is better if keep ourselves dump here for a moment, there is a spy somewhere and I do not want any one on the asteroid to know what is going on." Said Steve

"Good idea, I like the way you think, who knows how it works except you and engineering?" ask the Admiral.

"Only Dex and major Kick as they are now in charge of the mines at this moment sir." Said Steve

"Now the only problem is that ships that we do not know of that is in control of the enemy could get through the mine field that is why we are here sir, to stop them until we can program the mines with the new data, which action would only take a few seconds sir." Said Steve

"I like that very much Steve, now how many mines are there in total at this moment. Ask the Admiral.

"There are Two thousand deployed at ten light years from here and the total will be ten thousand in a few hours time Sir, with the most dense population at five years sir." Said Steve.

"That is wonderful Steve, we might just win the war the way we are going on." Said the Admiral

Just then one of the Generals came running out of the board room shouting.

"A ship has been destroyed ten light years from here Admiral, what is going on?"

"Is it one of our enemy ships that were destroyed general?" ask the Admiral

"Yes sir it was." replied the general

"Then you do not have to be concerned general, something is doing us a favor by attacking our enemies." Answer the Admiral

"Yes sir, that is another way of looking at it, but we are just concerned that we are next." Said the general

"Relax and enjoy the show general, we will worry about it when it starts attacking our fleet." Said the Admiral.

"Sir if you do not mind, everything is under control, I would like to get some sleep as I have been up for 36 hours non stop and are now worst for wear." Said Steve

"Sure Steve, contact me the moment you awake so that we could go over the next few steps that we need to take." Said the Admiral

"I will do so sir." said Steve and left.

Steve got to his quarters and fell on his bed and was almost asleep before he closed his eyes, he was awakening with soft wet kisses from Lydia, and slowly he started coming back.

"How long did I sleep." He asked

"Twelve hours, how are you feeling?" ask Lydia

"Still tired but wonderful now that you are here." Said Steve

"Clean up, and then I will get some food for us, some very interesting things has been happening around space the last couple of hours, you must see that." Said Lydia

"I think I know what you are talking about." Said Steve from the shower.

"Oh what do you know about the ships that keep on exploding with no reason what so ever?" ask Lydia

It is then that Steve realized that he better write a memo about the explosions as not to scare the fleet but rather to excite them, so they could realize that the war could be won without any casualties from our side, or so he hopes.

He got out of the shower and sat down in front of the computer and start to write the memo to the fleet, explaining to them that the mines were created in order for the war to end before it started and to minimize casualties on our side, if the mines are successful then it would not be long before everyone in the fleet can return to their homes and take a well deserve break

He then sent the memo to the Admiral for approval before it is sent to the fleet, as there is still the spy that they are looking for.

Lydia came and sat next to him at the desk, immediately realizing that he is still in the nude and she placed her hand high up on his leg.

"What do we have here?" she asks

"Work and pleasure don't mix well, but exceptions can be made." Answered Steve

At that moment the Admiral sent a message to Steve that he can go ahead with sending the memo and that they caught a spy on the asteroid and are currently working with her to see what the enemy knows, the asteroid's cover are blown as the enemy now knows about the asteroid.

Steve sent the message to the rest of the fleet, and then he asked.

"Lydia take your clothing of slowly, I need to look at you for a moment?"

She looked at him surprised but responded by taking off her top and then her bra, slowly she took off her pants and panties, then she stood in front of him totally naked, and he realized that her beauty is greater than what he could remember.

He softly stokes her breast as it is slightly swollen from pregnancy and her stomach is not showing yet, but he knows that it will soon start to show.

He laid her down on the bed and made love to her very softly and gentle, as he does not want her to get hurt.

His buzzer went mad and it woke him up in Lydia's arms, it was the Admiral.
He got dressed and kissed Lydia and left for the Admiral.

"Sorry I had to wake you Steve but it was necessary, I hope that you rested well as there is a lot of work to do." Said the Admiral
"I rested well sir." Said Steve
"Forty six enemy ships were destroyed by the mines in the last ten hours, the enemy is very confused as they do not know what is attacking them as the mines are rather small and they can not see them easily, the enemy did contact the spy and she told them that it is not from us, she does not know what is attacking them, she also told them that we are also investigating the matter." Said the Admiral
"Who is the spy?" ask Steve
"You won't believe it, it is the wife of one of the war generals, and we have both of them in custody as we can not take any chances at this point." Said the Admiral

"That is disturbing news sir, especially with the cover of the asteroid now blown it makes you a big target." Said Steve
"I do not think that it is so serious as they know for a while already, but to get back to the mines, one of our own ships got here from a very far mission and went pass a few of your mines and your mines did not fire on

them, this ships crew are now getting trained on the new weapon system." said the Admiral

"That is the way that the mines were programmed sir, I also programmed a self destruct device, incase the enemy tries to reprogram the mine to fire on us or bother with it in any way, I also programmed it to sent data to us incase there are ships approaching that we do not recognize so that we can add that type of ship to the list of enemy ships sir." Said Steve

"That is good thinking Steve, now let us go over the war strategy, we need to have some sort of plan for this war.' Said the Admiral

Steve and the Admiral worked for six hours solid on plans and backup plans, they moved ships into different positions around Astoria and Steve contacted Dex as the last of the plans.

"Dex move fifty mines around us and the asteroid so that we have ultimate protection just incase something gets through to attack us." Ordered Steve.

"Yes sir that is done." Said Dex

While they were looking at the star map they saw enemy ships being destroyed by the mines.

Then they saw what they have been expected to see, a huge fleet of enemy ships coming from all directions towards them, it looks like they have moved themselves into position outside of our monitors range, and then by a given command they moved in with speed all at the same time.

With ten thousand mines around the planet Steve was worried if that was going to be enough.

Steve spoke into the communication system to all the ship commanders at once.

"Prepare for battle code red, all ships fire at will." Ordered Steve

Some ships broke through the ten light year mine field as Steve expected as the area is vast and the mines were few. Coming towards them with speed that Steve did not expect,

Steve was worried if the mines would be able to pick and shoot them down at the speed the ships are doing.
At the five year mark Steve saw that the mines are responding well and one after the other the enemy ships exploded.

Steve saw that one of the enemy ships were hit but was not dead yet and were coming strait for the asteroid, but before Steve could give the order for his own ship to open fire, one of the mines he placed around him and the asteroid fired and the ship exploded.
Steve was relieved that the mines are successful and the planet is safe for the moment.

Another problem was staring Steve in the face, all the space debris is causing a problem for their own ships to maneuver through space, he had to think of something to remove this new problem so that they could clearly see where the next attack is going to take place.

Then he thought of something, the mines worked in the way that he gave each mine a serial number, now to use the transporter beam he lock on to the mine and give it another location, that is the way he move the mines around in space, now what if he give the debris a serial no, then it must work the same way.

With that in his mind he went to the bridge to find Dex and Kick in serious conversation.
"What seems to be the problem?" ask Steve

"The debris sir, we can not see what is coming towards us and that is a great concern." Said Dex.

"What we need to do is to give the group of debris a serial number and using the transporter unit, transport the debris to deep space where it won't be a problem for us anymore." Said Steve

"Brilliant plan Sir, Let us do it, where would you say is the safest place to place it sir?" ask Kick

Steve looked at the star map and decided that the maximum range for the transporter would only be ten light years from here but it would be out of the way.

"Select that zone ten light years from here to place all the debris there on one pile so that it would look like a scrap yard." said Steve

Dex gave the serial number to the group of debris closest to them and circles the debris, he then circle the area where it must go to and activate the transporter.

In an instant the space in front of them was clear and the debris was at the designated place.

"Excellent sir." said Dex

"Now I do not want you to do all the work as you do have the mines to control, I will transport to one of the other mother ships and train them what to do." Said Steve

"Sir with respect, I know how the system works let me go as I feel you are more of value here at this time." Said Kick.

Steve agreed and gave him a written memo for the mother ship.

Kick left to the other mother ship and Steve felt lonely and missed Lydia, he went to his quarters and she was not there.

"Computer please locate Lydia?" ask Steve

"Lydia is not on board the ship commander." replied the computer

"What do you mean she is not on board, where did she go?" ask Steve

"She left the ship two hours ago with two other people and transferred to the asteroid sir." Said the computer

Steve instantly knew that this is a disaster as Lydia would never leave the ship without consulting with him, she must have been forced or tricked. Steve went into her quarters and became ice cold when he saw a note on her bed. He took the note and read it.

"Your girl has been taken by us; if you want to see her alive again you must disarm all the mines and order the fleet to evacuate the planet. If not she will die the most horrible death and very slowly too. Signed Todd and wife.

Steve shook from the inside the shock and the idea of losing a second loved one in one war was to much for him to bear.

Steve transport himself to the asteroid to find the Admiral.

The Admiral was asleep when Steve got there and he had to wake him up.

"Sorry to wake you up Admiral, but Lydia have been kidnapped by our enemies." Said Steve and hand the Admiral the note.

"Oh no, that is terrible news Steve how did this happen?" ask the Admiral

"I am not to sure sir; all I know is that Todd is the war general that you have in custody for spying with his wife." Said Steve

"That is right, let us see what is going on." Said the Admiral

The Admiral picked up the communicator and contacted security.

"Is the general and his wife still in their sells?" ask the Admiral

A shock went through the Admiral, and Steve could see the concern on the Admiral's face when he closed the communicator.

"Two guards are dead and their sells are empty, they had outside help from inside the asteroid." Said the Admiral

"Computer, what is the position of the war general and his wife?" ask the Admiral

"They left the asteroid in a shuttle that was due to the planet. sir." said the computer

"Computer, did they go to the planet and were captain Loxton with them?" ask the Admiral

"They went past the planet and into deep space and yes captain Loxton were with them. Sir." said the computer

"Computer Can you track down where exactly they went." Ask the Admiral

"I have lost contact with them as they left the other side of the planet sir, as my vision is limited due to space debris. Sir." said the computer the Admiral activate the star map and Steve could see how the space was cleared from the debris and he could see the build up of scrap metal in the location he gave major Kick.

"How did this happen?" ask the Admiral

"I ordered the crew to give the debris a serial no and then use the transporter unit to move the debris to this location so that we have clear space sir." Said Steve

"That is brilliant Steve." Said the Admiral

"Computer can you establish captain Loxton's position in space?" ask the Admiral

"Negative sir she is out of range." Said the computer

The Admiral was very quite for a moment.

"You know Steve, we do not negotiate with enemies, and thinking of the lives of the people of the planet that we are protecting and the survival of this fleet, this is darn hard to say, but captain Loxton is now considering a casualty of war.

Steve was just looking down, he knows that the Admiral is right; to sacrifice one person for the lives of many is the right thing to do.

"I fully understand sir." Said Steve

"I am sorry Steve I can't imagine how you must be feeling at this moment. But I know it is hard." Said the Admiral

"Sir would you please excuse me, I think I would like to be alone for a short period of time, it is not easy to lose two loved ones in one war." Ask Steve

"That is fine Steve I will give you two days to consider your options. In the mean time I will see what I can do to get her back, if at all possible.

"Thank you sir." said Steve

Steve went back to his ship and went straight to his quarters. He took paper and pen and started designing. He completes the design in four hours. Then he went down to engineering.

"Commander on deck." Shouted one of the engineers as Steve entered.

"As you were, my friends how long will it take you to build this unit?" ask Steve

The engineers looked over the drawing and just whistle.

"What is this thing?" ask the engineer.

"This is a destroyer." Said Steve

"Self driven to a speed of one of our fastest ships, a mind of it's own, heat seeking object seeking and much more, this is a killer sir." Said the engineer.

"Yes it is. How long?" ask Steve.

"One day sir I have to get materials for this unit first sir." Said the engineer.

"Good contact me when you done I would love to test this unit." Said Steve

Then he went back to his quarters and thinking of Lydia what she must be going through. He fell asleep.

Steve did not sleep well, he was dreaming that he is falling then to wake up just before he hits the ground; he was shivering in cold sweat and just to fall asleep again with more nightmares to wake him up. He was dreaming that Lydia became a monster that want to consume him and spit him out as space debris, then his dream took a turn. He dream that there is a huge ship with dark sides and a bright light in the middle, it has fins at the back on the sided and a sharp nose, almost like an old fashioned submarine, just much wider and larger in size.

He the saw that Lydia was walking out of the shuttle craft just to dive back into the craft, with two people darting on after her, but she manage to close the door behind her and locked them out.

Then Steve woke up and was wide awake, that is the ship he was looking for, the command ship of the enemy. That is where Lydia is, he just hope that she does not do anything stupid. He knows now what to do, he is on his way.

His bleeper went mad and it was engineering.

Steve rushed down to engineering, and took a look at the destroyer.

It was looking better than what he thought, and he started with the simulation test on the unit. Every test he has done proved that the unit is working the way he designed it. Then he programmed the unit to not shoot that ship he dreamed about, but to protect itself from the fire from the enemy.

Steve then ordered engineering to continue to build this unit; he wants to have one hundred units by the same time tomorrow. Then he released the test unit into space and transferred himself to the Admiral.

Lydia was fast asleep when suddenly her door burst opened, and a man and a woman jumped on her bed. They tied her wrist up and gagged her as not to scream. "You are coming with us as our prisoner, any problems with you and I will not hesitate to kill you. Is that understood?" ask the man

"Good, then let us go." Said the man.

They went down to the cargo bay and transported to a building she did not know, the man was walking in front and suddenly stopped a person was waking in the alley and she recognize him as the Admiral, she wanted to scream but the woman put the laser gun to her forehead and showed her not to do anything.

They got to the shuttle bay and there was a shuttle ready to leave for the planet. The man walked up to the pilots and without a word shot them. They pushed her into the craft and took off. She could clearly see that the man who was piloting the craft is not a good pilot as he nearly bumped against the side of the asteroid as they came out of it.

Lydia knew that the shuttle is armed when she saw the all familiar keyboard and she knew that the man piloting the craft did not know this.

After a while flying to a destination she does not know. Lydia showed the woman to remove her mouth gag. The woman removed the gag.

"Who are you and why did you take me prisoner?" ask Lydia

"I am war general Todd and that is my wife Cindy, we are spies and were ordered to capture you so that your man can disarm the mines." Said the man.

"Steve would never do that, he would come after me, and when he does, you will be sorry." Said Lydia.

"We actually want him to follow us as there is a surprise party waiting for him at the other end." Said the general

"If you kill him, how is the mines going to be disarmed, as he is the only one that can do that?" ask Lydia

She could see how the general is thinking

"You know that there are spies like you within our ranks, Steve could not take the chance to let anyone but him control the mines that is the only way that the mines could be successful." Said Lydia.

"That could be true Todd." Said Cindy

"The fact that the mines are successful is true, it really put a hold on the war and our friends are leaking their wounds." said the general

Lydia saw how they go through the 10 light year minefield, the mines do not react to the shuttle as it is consider friendly.

Then she saw enemy ships in the distance, and she thought of something.

"Can you please loosen my hands, I need to use the toilet?" ask Lydia

The woman loosens her hands and she and Lydia went to the toilet. On their return she saw that they are being escorted, and she knew that Steve would never be able to get through the amount of enemy ships.

Lydia was sitting with her back towards the weapon controls and slowly without them noticing it she activate them and place it an automatic, she then rested and waited for the right time tom fire. Steve taught her well on the system and she is now glad that she concentrated on how the weapons worked.

Lydia saw how they are guided towards a huge ship that is long and wide with dark sided and a brilliant light on its back with fins on the side at the back. She never saw such a ship before, and she realizes that this must be the command ship of the enemy, the one Steve were looking for.

They went through the opening into the alien mother ship, they took turns and she tries to memorize all the turns but could not do so there were too many of them.

Then they landed on a circle in the middle of a huge opening and shut down, in front of her she saw the sign of high voltage and a lot of danger tokens, there was also a door that goes through the high voltage token, she realized that this is the power plant of the ship and that the hart of the ship must be not far off.

The general got up and started for the door, Lydia was not very eager to get out of the shuttle and the general had to pull her towards the door, his wife was already out of the shuttle, Lydia stopped resisting and the general got out of the craft first still holding her hand as to pull her out if she resist again.

Lydia pushed the general forward out of the door and he fell down the two steps to the floor. Lydia immediately shut the door behind her and ran to the armed weapon system.

She played the song that corrupt all the shields and then played the general song for mother ships, and then she fired straight into the power supply section of the ship.

The explosion that followed moved the shuttle back a few meters and she saw that the general and his wife did not survive the explosion.

She powered the shuttle up and turns the shuttle around then she fired again and again, the explosions were felt right through the ship.

She then moved the shuttle out of the clearing into the wall way they just came; people were running in all directions, and confusion was everywhere the ship was burning and all the lighting went out, the emergency light came on and then went out as well.

Lydia saw a door in front of her and she recognized the door as they came through it, she had to stop first so that the shuttle's night vision can zoom in, she saw the door and fired, the door exploded and then to her surprise she saw space on the other side of the hole.

Lydia know that she can not go out that opening as over fife hundred ships are waiting for her. So she lined up but waited. She then activated the ships emergency tracking device that will sent a signal through space one hundred light years from where she is.

This signal gives her exact position and she could be traced to where she is.

Then she waited, the ship around her is exploding and burning out of control and she realized that she killed the ship from the inside.

A enemy ship came into view and she could not risk being fired on so she fired at the ship and got a direct hit. The ship exploded in front of her. She moved away a bit so that the other ships can't see her clearly so they can't fire on her. But she was wrong, they fired into the burning ship and she had to withdraw to a safer distance from their onslaught. Suddenly she became scared; they are shooting at the command ship in order to explode the whole ship so that she would be killed at the same time.

Just then her ships comununicator came to life and Steve called her on it. "Lydia are you there?" ask Steve
"Yes Steve I am here, they are shooting at me, and I am hiding in the burning ship." Answered Lydia.
"Hold your position I am on my way, "Said Steve
She saw another ship in her line of fire so she fired on it and the ship exploded
She saw a piece of the burning ship broke away and explosions rip through the piece that broke off, she watch it disintegrates in front of her.

"Steve how far are you from me?" ask Lydia
"Not far now. What is your status?" ask Steve
"This ship is about to explode with me in it." Said Lydia
"Get out of that ship and move to the east as soon and as fast as you can." said Steve

She lined up for the opening but was greeted by enemy fire. Because of all the smoke she could not see them but she returned fire and at the same time moved her craft out of the burning ship, in the corner of her eye she saw how ships started exploding but she could not make out what is shooting at it. She turned east and opened the ships speed valves. At a moment she saw a thing shooting past her firing at enemy ships and the thing stayed with her firing all the time.

Then she saw another one like that coming from the other direction firing at enemy ships, she could not make out what this is, she never saw something like this before. But she is glad they are there and they are protecting her.

Suddenly they both turned around and disappeared into space. Frantically Lydia looked where they went and saw that they were chasing the enemy ships that has decided to make a run for it, one by one the ships were destroyed.

Then suddenly Steve appear next to her, his ship looked big and strong and Lydia started crying of relief and of the tension she was under, for the first time since the ordeal she thought of her child she was carrying and she could not help but to cry even harder.

"Lydia are you hurt?" ask Steve

"No just glad to see you, what took you so long?" ask Lydia

"I had to design and build the destroyers first," said Steve

"What is a destroyer?" ask Lydia

"Those things that you saw fighting the enemy are the destroyers." Said Steve

"I got a fright when I saw them, they look mean." Said Lydia

There was a moment silence.

"Lydia can you keep on this heading Dex will bring you in, there is something I need to handle right now. Said Steve

Lydia wanted to protest but then she saw the fighters from their mother ship coming towards them with the speed of light, and she knew that it means trouble.

Steve met up with them and they disappear into space.

"Captain Loxton please turn to three degrees starboard and prepares to dock." Said Dex

"Turning three degrees and coming in to dock." Said Lydia relieved that she is back on the ship.

Steve got to the Admiral just as he was getting ready to go to bed.

"Admiral I am sorry to disturb you, but I need to show you what I have designed and build in the last five hours." said Steve

"Let us have a look." Said the admiral.

The admiral just whistles when he saw the potential of the destroyer.

At that moment the computers lit up and you could clearly hear the emergency signal from the shuttle that Lydia was on. The Admiral presses the search button and the computer gave the exact position of the shuttle.

Without a word to each other Steve spoke to Dex

Dex please contact engineering and ask them how many destroyers are ready?" ask Steve

"What is a destroyer sir" ask Dex

"You will see soon." Said Steve with a smile.

"Sir Engineering says that they got one more ready Sir." said Dex

"Ok, Dex I want you to activate them and transfer them to the location of that signal, then sit back and watch the show." Said Steve

"Sir I would like your permission to go there myself to locate and find captain loxton

"Take some of your crew with you Steve we can not afford to loose you now." Said the Admiral

Steve transported to the craft and took of with speed when he was in space he contacted Dex

"Dex get the crew ready and meet me at the signal, I think that we need to score some more points." Said Steve

"Yes sir we are on our way." Said Dex eagerly

But Dex knew that he can not leave his post so he sent the fighters out under the command of major Kick, his second in command.

With them he also sent two new recruits to the crew for battle experience, as Dex felt that they need it the experience.

But then suddenly the mine radar alarm went of and did not stop screaming, Dex looked at it and had to react immediately.

Ships unknown to them has past the ten light-year mine field and is coming their way fast.

"Dex to Commander Holt". Dex called Steve

"Go ahead Dex". Said Steve

"There is some ships unknown to us coming through the mine field, heading for the planet' you will pick them up coming from the west." Said Dex

"I have got them thanks Dex." Said Steve

Steve called the squadron and diverted them to intercept the space crafts, his then change course to team up with them, as his craft were faster than theirs he arrived at his destination first and waited for the space crafts and his team.

The space crafts came to his position fast and he shot a burst of fire into space to stop them that is a warning signal generally known to stop oncoming crafts until communication is established.

The space crafts ignored his attempt, and Steve fired again but this time just missed them, in order to stop them as they were almost on top of him.

Then they responded by slowing down and going past him they stopped.

Steve gave a sigh of relief as he does not know who they were, at that moment the squadron arrived and fell in next to him.

Steve opened the general space communications channel and asked them who they were.

There was a moment of silence and then a voice that has been computer generated came through the speaker.

"We are from the group of planets called the Asphalt group of planets two hundred light years from here, our mission is to seek and destroy the Dakar as they destroyed two of our planets." Said the voice over the speaker.

"I am high commander Steve Holt from the inter galactic command and are protecting the planet from the Dakar, we are also at war from them.' Said Steve.

"We are not humanoids, but can we assist you in destroying the Dakar." Said the speaker.

Steve thought for a moment, "Computer, can you establish a link to their computer?" Ask Steve.

"Yes sir I have done so already." Said the computer

"Good, pull all their information that you can get from them and then sent them all the information that we have on the Dakar and also all the ships that is fighting for them." Said Steve.

"Yes you can, I want you to deploy ten light years from here, we will send you all the information of who is fighting with the Dakar and you can fight them from there Said Steve

"We just received the information, thank you we will look out for these ships." Said the Asphalt leader.

Steve ordered the team back to base and they withdrew from the Asphalts.

Steve pushed the craft to maximum speed to get back to Lydia, a lot of things went through his mind as he was traveling fast and the fleet came to close, Steve had to reverse in order to break in time or he would speed dangerously into the fleet. But his experience in flying saved his craft from colliding with one of the fleet's mother ships.

After docking Steve went to Lydia's quarters and found her in the bath sleeping, she had blue marks on her wrists and her eye was swollen and blue. He kissed her softly and that woke her up, then she kissed him tenderly and held him very tight.

"Don't you ever take your time again to rescue me, I was nearly dead, and I was so scared." Said Lidia, and she started shaking from delayed shock.

Steve knew he had to act fast as the baby was at risk.

"Not to worry my love, you are safe now, and I am glad I have met such a brave girl." Said Steve smiling.

"I had to escape from them; they would have killed me and our baby." Said Lydia crying

"They sure would have my love, but you did not give them a chance." Said Steve

Steve helped her out of the bath and helped her to get dressed, and then he contacted the medical department and asked them to give her a checkup.

Then Steve asked Dex to retrieve the video from the shuttle and to bring it to his quarters as the medical team was busy to give Lidia a checkup in her quarters and he did not want them to be disturbed.

Dex came into the quarters with the video.

"Thank you Dex, please view this with me as I am sure that we will learn something from our enemies?" asked Steve.

"Sure sir, it will be a pleasure." Said Dex and sat down on the chair next to Steve.

Together they looked at how the craft took off out of the asteroid.

"Wow what is that?" asked Dex

Steve pressed the pause button.

"What?" ask Steve

"It looked like the craft came out of the asteroid." Said Dex shocked

Steve then realized that Dex does not know that the asteroid is a camouflaged space craft.

"Dex what you see here and learn here is top secret and it does not leave the room." Said Steve.

"Sure commander." Said Dex

"The asteroid is where the Admiral is, it is the fleet's headquarters, and the asteroid is a fully functional space craft." Said Steve

"No wonder it follows us all the time. It will remain a secret sir." Said Dex

"Good let us carry on." Said Steve.

They came to a point where they could see the enemy ships closing in. At that time the doctor and Lydia came in to Steve's quarters.

"She is fine sir, the baby is doing well and mommy just needs a small rest and then she can resume her normal duties sir." Said the doctor

"Thank you doctor, I really appreciate you coming to see her." Said Steve

"No problem sir." Said the doctor and left

Lydia came and sat close to Steve while they looked at the shuttle came up to the fleet of enemy ships, then suddenly Steve froze.

"Go back a bit, please?" ask Steve

Dex went back a bit

"Stop right there." Said Steve

On the screen Steve saw one of the ships that are now stationed five light years out that claimed that they were enemies of the Dakar, and Steve instantly knew that they fooled him.

"Computer lock on to that ship and sent a signal to the whole fleet and to the mines and destroyers that they are not friendly but part of the enemy." said Steve

Steve activated the star map and they saw how the destroyers fire on the ships. Then to their horror they saw how their shields are holding and they returned fire, destroying six destroyers instantly. Then the enemy ships started moving towards the planet, shooting and destroying landmines as well as destroyers.

Steve had to act fast if he wants to stop them.

Steve opened the communication lines to the whole fleet.

"Red alert, all pilots scramble and shoot at will, try to concentrate your combined fire at one ship at a time." Ordered Steve

"Ship commanders keep one squadron at home to protect the mother ships, incase some of them get's trough." Said Steve over the intercom.

At that moment the Admiral came on line

"Steve what is happening?" ask the Admiral

"Those ships are part of the enemy sir, our weapons are not effective towards them sir, and they are coming to attack us right now sir." Said Steve

"Yes I can see that, did you notice that as we fire that their shields are actually pulsating, almost as if it is playing music themselves." Said the Admiral

"I did not notice that sir, but I do see what you mean sir, I will work on that for a moment." Said Steve

"While you do that I will come over to you, lets see what we can do, as we are going to suffer heavy losses if we do not solve that problem fast.' Said the Admiral

"I will be delighted sir." Said Steve

While Steve and his crew wait for the Admiral Steve studied the pulsating of the shields, and then he started to play the song they use on the table with his fingers, what makes it difficult is that he programmed the destroyers to change the song if the song is not effective, so he is trying to guess what song is playing. Then he got an idea.

"Computer gets the destroyers to play the fifth ballet of Mozart and concentrate on one ship only." Ordered Steve.

At that moment the Admiral walked in the room and sat down next to Steve.

The Admiral was looking very worried at that moment.

The destroyers started shooting the song at one ship and Steve played with them on the table, Steve could clearly see how the pulsating changed to counter the beat of the song.

"I have got it." Said Steve

"What have you got Steve?" ask the Admiral

"They are not playing music at all sir, what they are doing is to sent strong shielding out on the beat of our songs, so it blocks the notes to come through, and so the weapon is not successful against them sir." Explain Steve

"How do we fight that Steve?" ask the Admiral

Steve realized that the Admiral trust him and relied completely on him as he do not have a clue what to do.

"Wait and see sir, there is a few options, but I need to stop the fighters first before we take losses sir." explain Steve

"Good idea Steve." Said the Admiral.

"All pilots fall back to one light year from our position; do not engage with the enemy our weapons are not effective, we are working on the problem." Ordered Steve over the intercom.

They saw how the crafts turn around and came back to the one light year mark except for one craft that kept on speeding towards the enemy, Steve and the Admiral looked at disbelieve at how the craft ignored the order.

"Commanders please identify that craft and ask him to return to base immediately." Ordered Steve as the craft is within range of the enemy and could be destroyed.

One of the commanders came back to Steve.

"Sir it is one of our pilots, he is not responding, there might be a problem with his communication channel; we are trying to reach him by using other channels at the moment." Said the commander

"Keep on trying we do not want to loose him." Said Steve

At that moment the craft started firing on the enemy and they returned fire and the craft exploded in mid space.

"We have no chance against them at this moment, what other options do you have Steve?" ask the Admiral

Steve stood up and got a recording of music from his collection of music, he place it into the computer and started to play the music.

"Computer records this and sent it to the destroyers and links it to their weapons, and let them fire this music to the enemy." Said Steve

"That is done sir." Said the computer

Steve and the Admiral watched as the destroyers accepted the commands and started firing on the enemy.

They saw how the enemy craft started breaking up and then exploded with debris flying through space.

The excitement of every one in the room was a very welcome sight for Steve as this was the last resort, he had no other plan, they were doomed if this did not work.

"Computer sent this to the fleet." Ordered Steve between the noise

"That has been done sir." Said the computer.

"All pilots attack and shoot at will hunt them down and remember the highest score wins a holiday." Ordered Steve.

The crafts sped away with intention and Steve just smiled as he knows what the pilots are feeling and thinking

"Excellent Steve, what music did you use that were so successful?" ask the Admiral

"Jazz sir," said Steve with a smile

"Jazz! I don't understand, how the other music could not do so?" ask the Admiral confused.

"Sir the enemy are not human, and what they did was to sense the beat of the music and the flow of the sound the lasers carry, them they adjust the shields to counter our attack.

With jazz it is different as there is no set pattern for them to adjust to, therefore our success." Explain Steve

"That is brilliant." Said the Admiral

They saw how the enemy crafts spit out fighters to counter our attack and how our crafts fall into attack formation,

The fight has began and crafts were exploding everywhere, Steve could not make out if they are having losses as well, but that is to be expected as in war there is always losses on both sides, that is why Steve hated war so much, as he is a peaceful man that wants the best of every thing for everyone, specially the one's he love so much.

Steve took the Admiral away from the fighting on the screen and softly spoke to him.

"Admiral, with your permission, after the war, could you please marry me and captain Loxton?" ask Steve

"Naturally commander, it would be my greatest pleasure." Said the Admiral with a wide smile.

"Thank you sir, but keep it quiet I did not asked her yet?" said Steve secretly

"No problem let us win this war first." Said the Admiral

They went back to the scene and Steve saw that they are starting to win as the other ships are pulling away and are heading for deep space.

"They are running." Said the Admiral

"Yes sir they are, it is time to withdraw." Said Steve and took up the communication microphone.

"Is it not a bit premature Steve?" ask the Admiral

"No sir, we have twenty five destroyers ready to be transferred right now to finish them of. Sir." Said Steve

"Now that is good thinking, go ahead commander." Said the Admiral

"Computer. Transfer the destroyers in between the enemy craft and activate them." Ordered Steve

"Transfer complete sir and activated." Said the computer

Steve and the Admiral watch as the destroyers took over and the one after another enemy craft started to explode.

"All pilots return to base immediately, well done to all of you." Said Steve

"All commanders sent a loss and damage report to me within two hours from now, and keep some pilots on stand by incase of a counter attack." Ordered Steve.

"You will make a brilliant Admiral Steve." Said the Admiral

"Thank you sir, you were the one who taught me these tricks. Said Steve

"Not all of it, most of it is your leadership material and your personality." Said the Admiral

"Thank you sir." Said Steve

Steve took the inter ship phone and dialod the mess.

"Prepare for a lot of noisy pilots, and free for all." Said Steve

"Dex I want you to personally welcome the pilots back and prepare the loss and damage report." Said Steve

"Yes sir, it was wonderful to see you back in action sir, I have learned a lot." Said Dex

Steve looked around to see where Lydia was and could not find her.

"Dex where is Lydia?" asked Steve

"She left and scrambled with the other pilots when you ordered so, sir." Said Dex

Steve went lame with shock, he did not want her to go, but then he realized that she followed orders and he did not stop her. To be truthful he did not even thought of her at the time, as he was really very busy

"Computer, can you look if captain Loxston is between the pilots returning?" ask Steve with a little unsure tone in his voice.

"Yes sir she just docked." Said the computer

"Thank you." Said Steve

The Admiral taps Steve on the shoulder.

"One hell of a lady you have got there Steve, she went against doctors orders, he told her to keep it quiet for a few days." Said the Admiral with a smile

"Yes sir I think she will call this a quiet time sir." Said Steve with a smile

"Good luck with the debriefing later today, I am returning to my ship now to rest and to hear all the stories." Said the Admiral

"Stories there are going to be plenty sir, the biggest one that they do not know about is that we almost lost the war sir." Said Steve

"Thank you once again for not allowing that to transpire Steve." Said the Admiral

"All the thanks to Jazz sir, a great battle was won with jazz sir, we should treasure that beautiful piece of music forever." Said Steve.

"You are right, I will write something to that effect, maybe you could make a song about it and then we all sing it to motivate each other." Said the Admiral

"That is a excellent thought sir, leave that to me." Said Steve with a smile

Just then Lydia burst into the door, saluted when she saw the Admiral.

"I am back commander." Said Lydia very proud of her self.

"I am relieved that you are back my love, you must tell me everything." Said Steve holding her close to him

"I am off," said the Admiral and left

"Now Lydia I actually wanted you to stay and you went against doctors orders, what were you thinking?" ask Steve

"You gave the order all pilots must scramble and you were busy at the time so I went." Explained Lydia

"I was just worried that you could get hurt." Said Steve

"Don't worry my love, I got four little ships and a good shot at a mother ship as well, but I must be honest Steve, I was scared and was relieved when the destroyers took over." Said Lydia

"I am glad it is over, this war took its toll on me and everyone." Said Steve

Their conversation was interrupted by the cheers and noise from the mess as the pilots has something to celebrate and a lot to talk and brag about.

Steve took op the phone and dialed Dex.

"Dex gets the technical personnel to recover all the video tapes and replace them with new ones. All the tapes must come to my quarters so that we could review who had the most kills for the competition." Said Steve

"Come let us join the fun in the mess, I would love to hear some of the stories." Said Steve

"Ok I think that will be great, but not to long I am a bit tired." Said Lydia
"Are you sure you are ok?" ask Steve
"Yes I am just a bit tired, there was a lot of action these last twenty four hours and very little sleep." Said Lydia
"That is true, we will only be a short wile." Said Steve

They arrived at the mess and the noise was almost unbearable, as they walked in someone shouted.
"Commander on the deck."
Suddenly the room went quiet and every one jump to attention, one officer saluted, and Steve saw that some of them still had some drinks in their hands, but today he would not do anything about that.
"As you were." said Steve and let Lydia to an open table in the one corner.

The noise came back, and one of the pilots came over to Steve.
"Sir if I may, can I congratulate captain Loxton here." Said the pilot
"Sure what for?" ask Steve
"As we came up to the enemy crafts, one of the little fighters came out of the mother ship and fired on the captain, she then turned and shot him back into the mother ship and kept on shooting until the craft exploded, causing multiple explosions in the mother ship.

I think she was the reason that the mother ship exploded." Explain the pilot

Steve looked at Lydia, she was just smiling and did not say a word.

"I that case thank you for sharing it with me, we will review the tapes later today and remember that the competition is still on and may the winner enjoy his or her prize." Said Steve

The pilot went back to his table

"Was that true?" ask Steve

"Yes I shot him back into his ship and then shot three others as well." Said Lydia

"Congratulations then my darling, you are one brave woman." Said Steve

After a few drinks Steve saw a nurse that checked Lydia out when she came back from her ordeal with the general, Steve called her over.

"Yes sir is every thing in order?" ask the nurse

"Yes every thing is fine, but what I would like you to do is to take the captain to her quarters, see that she is ok, as she needs some rest, will you do that for me please?" ask Steve

Lydia looked at him with surprise, and he held her softly

"There is some things I need to do and I would join up with you soon, but work now comes first." Said Steve

"Ok I understand," Said Lydia

She left with the nurse and Steve could see the tiredness in her, being pregnant and little sleep is not good at all. He feel sorry that he dragged her here, she much rather want to spent time with him, but plenty time later he thought and left the mess room for the bridge.

Dex was on the bridge scanning space for any hostile crafts.

"Sir I have sent a patrol of two crafts out to do a 360 at five light years to see if any enemy crafts still exist, so far nothing but debris." said Dex

"That is good." Said Steve

"Did the loss and damage reports come through?" ask Steve

"Yes sir, I did not have a look at it yet sir, but here they are." Said Dex and gave them to Steve.

Steve went through the reports and then started to summarized them for the Admiral

"We lost seven pilots and forty four ships were damaged. "Said Steve to Dex

"We came of light sir." Said Dex

"Yes it could have been worse, much worse." said Steve

Steve write down the names of the pilots who perished and then he sent it to the Admiral as it is his duty to let their families know of their death, a job that he hates to do, but thank goodness it is for the Admiral.

"We have to clean up this mess in space. Dex can you remember which ship did the initial clean up?" ask Steve.

"Yes sir they are already busy cleaning up sir." Answered Dex

"I want you to assign two more ships to help with the clean up, let us get it done soon as there it a lot of people that wants a break after the war." Said Steve

"You are right there sir, I know of two mother ships that were in space now just over two years without a break sir.' Said Dex

"I am going to the Admiral now, I will let him know, and it is time for them to return to their planet." Said Steve

"The video tapes are in your quarters as you ordered sir," said Dex

"Thank you Dex we will study it together later, I need to see the Admiral and then get some rest." Said Steve

"That will be fine sir." Said Dex

Steve arrived at the Admiral just as he was getting ready to go to sleep

"Admiral sorry to disturb you sir," said Steve

"No problem Steve, how can I help you?" ask the Admiral

"Sir it came under my attention that some of our ships have been in space for a long time some as long as two years." Said Steve

"Wow I was not aware of that Steve, I think you must draw up a list of who has been in space the longest and then sent them home." Said the Admiral

"It would be my pleasure sir, have a good night sir, I am also going to rest now." Said Steve

"Good, contact me when you are awake then we talk more." Said the Admiral

"Will do so sir." Said Steve and return to his ship.

Steve wrote a memo to the fleet, requesting the amount of time spent on this mission in space without a break. He then went to sleep; he did not want to disturb Lydia as she was very tired.

Steve woke up by wet kisses from Lydia, she was bending over him completely naked and dripping wet, he could see the bulge in her stomach and the swelling in her breast as she was kissing him.

"Wake up my love I need to talk to you." Said Lydia

"With what you are wearing my love you does not have to say a word." said Steve

She giggled and got in bed with him all wet and Horney

Much later Steve looked at the information that came through from the ships and soon realized that over half of the fleet was in space for more than two years without a break and the fleet policy states. Clearly that except for war times, no person may be in space away from his home for more than one year at a time. That is done so that families could flourish and prosper.

War is now over and Steve written a memo to the fleet that as soon as the awards has been given to the winning pilots that some ships may depart for home, he will give the orders soon.

Steve contacted Dex to come to the boardroom to evaluate the video tapes.

Dex arrived at the boardroom with snacks and drinks on a tray and Steve raised an eyebrow.
"Not to worry commander, it is movie time and snacks are for free." Said Dex with a smile.

Steve just smiled as that is what he likes so much about the man, he always thinks ahead and his plans are as original as is his personality.
"Good thinking Dex I did not eat for a long time, shall we start with captain Loxton when she was captured?" ask Steve
"Good choice sir, that was about the beginning of the war." Said Dex

They forward the tape to the point where she entered the alien mother ship, they saw how she fired on the electrical units and how it exploded, throwing the craft a few feet backwards, they saw how she turned and shot the wall and it exploded out into space, then they saw how a craft came into view and shot at her and how she returned fire and the craft exploded.

As she exit the craft they actually saw at the background how the mother ship starting to disintegrate with explosions from her attack.
Steve made a note.
"One command mother ship and one fighter." Said Steve
"Confirmed. "Said Dex
"She is one hell of a brave lady." Said Dex
"That is true, she surprises me each day." Said Steve

Steve took the next tape on the pile and start rolling eating snacks and drink cold drink while the worked. It was a couple of hours before they were finished.
"Ok Dex I need to confirm with the Admiral, and I will let you know how we are going to announce the winners, as there is more than one winner here, and Dex not a word to anyone, not even to my lady." Said Steve
"No problem sir." Said Dex

Steve went to the Admiral's office and the Admiral was in a conversation with head office so Steve did not enter until the Admiral completed the conversation.

"Steve please come in, I see that you have papers in your hand, what news do you have?" ask the Admiral.
Steve could sense that the Admiral is in a particular good mood.
"The pilot scores sir, a interesting result sir." Said Steve
"Let us have a look at it." Said the Admiral

Steve and the Admiral discuss the result and came to a decision and then decided that a live video to all ships is the best way to present the results.

Steve sent a memo that all crew members of the entire fleet to be in their boardrooms in one hour from then for the prize giving, as it is going to be presented by the Admiral himself over live broadcast.

Steve returned to his ship to prepare for the broadcast

Lydia found him in his quarters taking a shower and saw that his full tunic is laid out on the bed.

"What is going on?" she asks

"I have to be with the Admiral to do the presentation of the winner's prize." Said Steve

"That sounds nice, may I came with?" ask Lydia

"I wish you could, but you will see me on video, and there are a few surprises in store, you will see soon." Said Steve

"What is it I want to know?" insist Lydia

"Sorry girl, I may not speak about it." Said Steve as he got dressed

"Ok I get it, you won't tell me, but that is ok, I will find it out soon enough on the video." Said Lydia mockingly

"Yes you will, can you please help me with the sash?" ask Steve

"No, first tell me!" insist Lydia

"You woman are always so curious, ok I will tell you this bit but that is all." Said Steve and kept quiet

"Come on Steve you are killing me." Said Lydia now almost angry

"There is a surprise for you, but I am not saying what." Said Steve

"Oh I love surprises, I could not wait on my birthdays to get the presents, then I open them slowly as to not spoil the moment, I love it." Explain Lydia

"Typical woman, now help me here?" ask Steve

She help him to fit the sash around his waist, the sash is a recommendation of extra orderly service to the fleet and only high commanders who earned it may wear it. It is like a medal but worth much more as it only are worn on special full dress uniform, and demands respect by all ranks.

"I did not know you had one of these Steve." Said Lydia

"Yes I got it about ten years before after the war with the Dalian's." Said Steve

"Who are they?" ask Lydia

"You mean who were they?" said Steve

"How do you mean, were they?" ask Lydia

"No time to explain the details, but they were a race that went out to destroy planets for the fun of it, like pirates, looting raping woman then torture them before killing them." Said Steve

"What did you do?" ask Lydia

"Wipe them completely out of existence that was the only way." Said Steve.

"Oh gruesome." Said Lydia pulling a face

"I am off to the Admiral, you behave now you hear." said Steve and ran out of the door

On the way to the cargo bay Steve walked past some crew and pilots, when they spotted him they jump on to attention and all of them saluted, one of them said as he was past.

"I never saw the sash in my life before, the commander is really something."

Steve just smiled as he knows that only about thirty officers have a sash, it is very rare to see one, he himself only saw one when he received it, so it is really special.

Steve met the Admiral already sitting in front of the camera. The Admiral does not have a sash.

The Admiral looked at Steve and knotted in approval.

"Now that looks nice have a seat here next to me, we are doing this together." Said the Admiral

"Now sit so that the fleet can see your sash, you deserved it and to be frank with you, you deserve another one for this war." Said the Admiral

Steve just looked at the Admiral and repositioned himself so that the sash is visible to the camera.

"Did you ask her to marry you yet?" ask the Admiral

"No not yet sir there was just not enough time to do so." Said Steve

"Well you will have to do it tonight as we are all leaving tomorrow, I tell you what when we have a moment I will open the channel and you can ask her." Said the Admiral

Before Steve could answer the camera started rolling.

"Good evening to every body in the fleet. As you know we promised a nice holiday for the person with the most kills in the fleet, all expenses paid. And so it will be done but before we come to that, there is a few other pleasant surprises and I must say I am pleased with the result that we as a fleet accomplished these past couple of days." Said the Admiral. After a small pause.

"Commander Holt, without you we would never have won this war, your skill and intelligent way of thinking put a new way of fighting in the history books of the fleet.

The headquarters awarded the highest recommendation to you and their appreciation for the work you have done. You are now promoted to the rank of Admiral from effect immediately." Said the Admiral

"Can you kneel down please commander." Ask the Admiral

Steve was so shocked about the news it took him several seconds to realize what is happening, he kneeled down in front of the Admiral

The Admiral took out his sword and touches the shoulders of Steve

"With this I swore you in at the rank of Admiral, your duties is going to be in charge of the training academy and in charge of the new technology centre they are now building for you." Said the Admiral

"You may stand up Admiral." Said the Admiral

"Thank you sir" said Steve

A captain came forward and removed Steve's old rank and replaced them with his new rank

"Captain Loxton, could you please stand up" ask the Admiral

The camera in the ship came to life and Steve could see Lydia standing up between the crew, she was sitting next to major Kick

"Please captain walked over to the camera so that we could all see you?" ask the Admiral

Lydia came forward and she never looked as beautiful as now to Steve

"Now captain Loxton was captured by our enemies and escaped from their hands blowing up their command mother ship in the process. She also took one of their fighters out on the way out. Then she ignored doctor's orders as she is pregnant with the Admirals child, and scrambled with the other pilots to attack the enemy, where she took out another mother ship and four small fighters." Said the Admiral

Lydia was just standing there smiling

"Captain you are now being promoted to the rank of major and will be giving training to pilots at the academy as you showed no fear and showed us all how it must be done. Well done major." Said the Admiral

"Thank you Admiral." Said Lydia loud and clear

"Now major, the Admiral here next to me has something to share with you." Said the Admiral

Steve looked at the Admiral in disbelief, but took the challenge.

"Major Loxton, congratulations with your new rank, but that is not what I am supposed to do, please wait a second?" ask Steve

Steve then stood up from behind the table, walked forward and went to his knees.

"Major Loxton would you please be so kind to become my wife and partner for the rest of my life. As I love you dearly and want to marry you?" ask Steve

Lydia was taken by surprise, and was just looking to the screen in disbelief, someone in the audience shouted to her.

"Say yes! we want to party."

Then she started laughing

"Yes Admiral I will marry you" said Lydia

A loud cheering was heard across the fleet the Admiral had to lift his hand to silence the fleet.

"There will be a wedding ceremony at the chapel of the Admirals ship shortly after this meeting" announce the Admiral with a smile

"now for the best score in the fleet Major Loxton did score the highest as she took out the command ship of the enemy, but we could not count that as the fighting did not begin yet, although that was the beginning of the war.

We looked at all the videos and all the pilots had some kills, and that made me proud to see the experience you picked up in doing so." Said the Admiral

"We also had some losses, seven pilots died fighting this war, they were your friends and we are sad to see them off, but we came of light this time, I actually thought for a moment that we are going to loose this battle. But luckily the Admiral had a plan and it worked, cutting our losses to seven. Well done Admiral and well done to all of you." Said the Admiral

"The pilot with the highest score, is a man with no battle experience, he shot down twenty two small crafts and then manage to take out three mother ships. Airman Gunter, would you please stand up?" request the Admiral

A young skinny boy not more than twenty stood up slowly, red in the face as he did not expect this.

"AIRMAN YOU DID FANTASTIC." Said Steve with a big smile

"Thank you sir." Said the airman shyly.

"Now you are going to a planet in the fifth zone of the Zodiac and you can take your parents, your girlfriend and her parents to the resort for a month, all expenses paid by the fleet as we have promised." Said the Admiral

"Thank you sir, I appreciate that sir." Said the Airman

"We appreciate what you have done more, so much more that we have decided that you get promoted to full lieutenant from effect immediately." Said the Admiral

That information was to mush for the airman, he fainted right there on the spot. The Admiral and Steve looked at each other and just burst out laughing, it takes about ten years to reach the rank of second lieutenant and then another four to get to full lieutenant.

This airman is in the fleet only six years and was never on a mission before

Two medics came to him and took him out of the room; his mates were clapping hands as he left the room.

"Now the second highest score was a lady with some experience as she completed a couple of missions before, she took out three mother ships and two fighters, her ship was damaged and she had to return to her ship, it wasn't for that she most properly would have won this reward. She took heavy enemy fire and did not back off." explain the Admiral

"Will Captain Finn please stand up?" request Steve

A middle aged woman stood up and straitens her hair with her fingers; Steve studied her and saw the strength within her, a quality that is not rare between the woman fighters of the fleet. The woman competes with men in the fleet and they learn quickly to fight for themselves. Lydia has the same quality in her and that is what made her do what she did when she was captured.

"Captain the fleet recognize the skill and dedication that you showed in the attack, and awarded you with a holiday for two people in the resort of your choice, also it came to our attention that you applied for a position at the training school, so that you could be closer to home as your parents are aging and you wanted to be close to them." Said Steve

"Yes sir" she replied

"We have therefore decided to let you go with major Loxton to the academy to train the other pilots the skill and determination you just showed us." Said Steve

"Thank you sir." Said the woman

"Furthermore, you are also promoted to the rank of major, congratulations major." Said Steve

"Thank you sir, thank you very much." Said the woman smiling

"Now there is just one more person who stood out right from the start of the war until it was all over." Said the Admiral

"This person was hitting the enemy hard and really fought his way through, he took out thirty fighters and wounded a mother ship in such a way that it could not function any more, the destroyers then finished him off. The reason the destroyers took the mother ship is because this pilot was hit badly and is one of the seven pilots that tragically did not make it." Said the Admiral.

"He was a married man with children and the fleet will compensate them accordingly. We are sad to loose such a great man and pilot," said the Admiral

'Now for some good news, the fleet that is here right now is to return to our home base immediately and every one is on leave with full pay for six months as soon as we get there. From there on new missions will be assigned and you all will be back in space again. You has proven your dedication to the fleet and we appreciate all that you have done, therefore the long leave for every one." Said the Admiral

Cheers went through the fleet.

"This meeting is over, you may leave as soon as you are ready but keep at least a quarter light year between ships as we do not want any accidents now due to recklessness, keep the discipline strong in place at all times." Said the Admiral. The screen went dead.

Steve and the Admiral shook hands.

"I will see you at the chapel in one hour Steve." Said the Admiral

"One hour will be fine sir that will get Lydia time to prepare." Said Steve

"Let her dress up in full dress uniform and you stay as you are." Said the Admiral

"That is fine sir I will also get the guys to video the ceremony for our records." Said Steve

With that they oach went their own way.

Steve found Lydia in her quarters; she was sitting on her bed crying. Steve put his arms around her and held her tight.

"What is the matter my love?" ask Steve

"My stomach is to big to fit into the tunic." she cried

Steve looked at her stomach and smiled, for the first time he could see how she has grown with pregnancy, and he loved her even more

"No problem my love I will handle it for you." Said Steve

Steve ran to his quarters and dialed the store master.

A man with the name agmed answered the phone

"How can I help you sir." Ask the man.

"Agmed, do you have woman tunics in your store?" ask Steve

"Yes Admiral I do have, not a lot but there is some." Said Agmed

"I am bringing the major to you now let her fit some on." Said Steve

"I will be waiting for you sir." Said Agmed

Steve dialed the bridge and ordered for a lady orderly Clark to come to Lydia's quarters immediately.

Steve went back to Lydia, she was lying on her bed eyes all swollen from crying

"It has been handled, we are going to the store room and you can fit some tunic's on till you get one, do not worry about the Admiral I will stall him a bit." Said Steve holding her hand

"Thank you, congratulations on your rank Admiral." Said Lydia

"Thank you my love it was somewhat unexpected at the time." Said Steve

"I loved the way you asked me to marry you, when you kneeled down I was not sure if you had a cramp in your stomach or what was going on." Said Lydia now smiling

"Yes the sash makes it awkward to kneel down, but I did it." Said Steve

A knock on her door.

Steve opened the door and a very pretty lady stood there, not sure why she is there, she saluted Steve

Steve saluted back.

"I want you to take major Loxton to the store, and help her to fit on a tunic that she is comfortable in. we are getting married and she must look beautiful, so do some make up then bring her to the chapel." Said Steve

"Sure Admiral it would only be a pleasure sir." Said the girl

Lydia went with the girl and Steve went to the bridge.

"Everything in order here ?" ask Steve

"Yes Admiral, the first lot of ships has departed already sir." Said Dex

"Just check their following distances, like that one there is to close, ask him to hold back a bit." Said Steve

Dex contacted the ship and Steve could see how the ship is slowing down to the correct distance.

"I guess they are all in a hurry to get home sir." Said Dex

"Sure they are. We will be departing soon as well, I need you to leave five destroyers with the planet, then sent the rest of them with the ships as they depart. The destroyers are the defense incase they ran into more trouble." said Steve

"Shall I transfer destroyers to the ships that have gone sir?" Ask Dex

"Yes do that and let them know that we are doing it for their safety." Said Steve.

"What about the mines sir?" ask dex

"I will order them to self destruct." Said Steve

Steve keyed in coordinates into the computer and then all the mines exploded in mid space.

"That was quite a show Admiral." Said Dex

"I have been expected something like that, check and see that all the mines did go off, we do not want any accidents." Said Steve

"Will do so sir." Said Dex

Steve contacted the media group and asked them to shoot a video of the ceremony at the chapel.

"How will the people of this planet know how to use the destroyer's sir?" ask Dex

"The Admiral has sent all the data down to the defense section of the planet, as well as the plans to build their own." Said Steve

"That is good thinking sir." Said Dex

Steve's buzzer went of, it was Lydia looking for him.

Steve rushed to her quarters and found her and the lady doing make up

"Steve we could not find anything in the store that will fit, but I have found a very nice old fashion dress that will do the trick, may I use it instead?" ask Lydia

"Under these circumstances I would say yes my dear, now get dressed I will meet both of you at the chapel." Said Steve and ran to the chapel as he has to stall the Admiral.

Steve got to the Admiral just as he entered the chapel and quickly talked to him.

"Admiral, due to her pregnancy Lydia could not find any tunic that fits over her stomach, she found an old fashion dress instead. Would that be in order sir?" ask Steve

"Naturally Steve, I actually forgot that she is pregnant." Said the Admiral

"Yes I noticed that she suddenly ballooned out, she was not big yesterday, but today it really shows." said Steve

"I take it that she will be a little late then." Said the Admiral

"Yes I presume so sir, there is something else I was thinking off, I have no family but she has her mom and dad, would it be possible that they can come with us and live with us at the academy?" ask Steve

"Yes I was to ask you about that, it is fine as you get house no D ten that is the house with five bedrooms and a three bedroom flat with its own entrance. Her parents can stay in the flat." Said the Admiral

"Just after the ceremony our ship will depart sir, we will go and collect her son and the parents will have to pack as well, so that we can transfer their goods before the ship go out of range , sir. Said Steve

"That will give you three day's for them to pack, will that be enough time Steve?" ask the Admiral

"It has got to be sir, I am not holding our ship back for them, as every one on board wants to go home sir." Said Steve

"Yes that is right, the asteroid is just waiting for the ceremony then we will be off too." Said the Admiral

At that moment the chapel was getting full with pilots and crew and every one gasps as Lydia and the orderly Clark came in to the chapel, photos flash and the video started recording.

Lydia looked stunning she wore a wide skirt with layers and layers of material that looked like a waterfall from the hip down to the ground, you could not see her feet at all, her top was loose around her stomach and it was a low cut so that the top part of her swollen breast were showing, her hear was done up and her make up was done expertly.

Steve always knew that she was beautiful, but today he saw exactly how beautiful she really is. A tear of joy and appreciation roll down his face he had to wipe it off with the back of his hand.

Steve looked at the Admiral, he was standing there with his mouth open with surprise, and he saw Steve looking at him.

"She looks magnificent Steve, the most beautiful bride I ever married, you are one lucky man." Said the Admiral as she walked down the aisle.

The Clark that brought her in also looked stunning, her blond hair was loose and falls over her shoulders, and her make up was done so that her blue eyes stood out, she was also a very attractive woman, thought Steve. Some of the pilots also think so, as Steve could see the stares she is getting, and he heard one of them saying.

"Who is she, I never saw her before she is gorgeous."

Then someone touches Steve's arm, it was Dex

"You need a witness sir, is it ok if I can have the honors sir?" ask Dex

"I would appreciate that Dex, I did not even think of that." Said Steve

"She looks stunning sir." Said Dex

"I am glad that I am marring her and not some other bloke, she knocks my feet from under me every time I looked at her, and being pregnant makes her glowing and even more attractive than ever before." Said Steve

"You are right there sir, you are a lucky man sir." Said Dex

"Thank you." Said Steve as Lydia reached them.

Steve took her in his arms and softly kissed her on the lips.

"You look stunning." Said Steve

"Thank you." Said Lydia

The Admiral took his place in front of them and gave a big smile at them.

"Today we are here to witness two people combining their lives together into one in marriage, I have witness the love they shared over these couple of months and are convinced that they are meant for each other as their love is of the purest and deepest I have seen in my career at the fleet.

If any one in this room has any doubts or reason why they should not marry then speak up now or forever keep you peace." Said the Admiral and kept silence as he scans the room for anyone who wanted to object. There was no one.

"Admiral Holt, do you promise that you will look after this woman, in sickness and in health, in richness and poor, do you promise to give her pots and pans, a bed to sleep in that is comfortable a good solid house to live in and a sane and peaceful environment?" ask the Admiral

"Yes I do." Answered Steve

"Do you also promise to love her children and to educate them the ways of living the ways of doing things and to bring them up to adulthood?" ask the Admiral

"Yes I do." Answered Steve

"Major Loxton, do you promise to love the Admiral is sickness and in health, in richness or poor, do you promise to keep his house in order, to be the one cleaning up after him, to clean up after his children?" ask the Admiral

"Yes I do." Said Lydia

"Do you promise to support him with the upbringing of your kids, support him in his work and to love him no matter what life will bring to you?" ask the Admiral

"Yes I will." Said Lydia

"Now to both of you, do you swear that you will abide by the rules to be mates for the rest of this lifetime. The rules are simple but effective.

1. Be faithful to each other, even when one partner is in space on a mission for a long time.
2. Do not speak negative about your partner to others.

3. Do not dishonor your partner in any way.
4. To sort out any problem with each other in a sane and peaceful manner, if that does not work seek professional help to solve the problem, the other partner must obey.
5. To stand by each other, support each other and to follow each other's path's how difficult it may seem.
6. To love each other unconditionally.

"Admiral Holt how do you answer to this?" ask the Admiral
"Yes I do." Said Steve
"Major Loxton how do you answer?" ask the Admiral
"Yes I do." Said Lydia

"Then by the power of the Supreme Being, and the power the fleet has invested in me, I declare you man and wife, and partners for life. No one but death can separate you now from this bond." Said the Admiral
"You may kiss the bride and take her away on your mission in life, God bless you both." Said the Admiral
Steve kissed Lydia very passion fully and felt her tears on his face mixing with his own tears.
The crowd went mad, they were jumping up and down and shouting, and yeah it's party time
The Admiral gave Lydia a kiss and shook Steve's hand
"Congratulations and we see you at the academy." Said the Admiral and left.

Dex came to Steve.
"Congratulations Admiral, it was the nicest wedding I ever experienced." Said Dex

"Thank you Dex, you must depart now and stay with the Admiral just in case he needs assistance, the major and I will join with you in three day's time, please prepare quarters for her parents and space in cargo hold no 1 as we are transferring their good to here." Said Steve

"Are they coming to live with you at the academy?" ask Dex

"Yes, the Major and they do not know about it yet, that is just another surprise for all of them." Said Steve.

"And what a surprise it is going to be, you know sir you can sometimes be full of it, and I like it a lot." Said Dex smiling

"Ok then get ready to move out." Said Steve and went to Lydia where she is standing talking to her friends.

"Come my love we must collect your son, I will not leave without him." Said Steve

"Really, can he come and live with us?" ask Lydia now smiling

"Yes my love he is now part of our family, did you not listen to the Marriage rules?" ask Steve

"Yes I did but I thought it is meant for this one and the rest to come." Said Lydia slightly confused

"Remember the words, "the upbringing of her children," can you remember it?" ask Steve

"Yes I do, thank you Steve you are wonderful, when do we leave?" ask Lydia

"Right now, this ship is departing now for home, and we have to catch it and dock at high speed." Said Steve

"That is dangerous," said Lydia

"Extremely, but not for me, I have done so many times." Said Steve

Together they rushed to Steve's ship. As it is the fastest ship on board, but no body knows that, it has been kept a secret all along for security reasons.

They entered space almost at the speed of light and Lydia had to hold on when Steve entered the atmosphere of the planet.

"Are you not scared to break up going in so fast?" Ask Lydia.

"Any other ship might break up, but not this one, it was specially designed for me to enter fast and to leave fast." Said Steve

"Yes we have to harry up our ship is leaving." Said Lydia.

At that moment Steve leveled out and correct to the direction of her parent's home

The ship's computer came on line

"Commander the air traffic police is trying to disable us but I have blocked their signal." Said the computer

"Computer sent the signal back and disables them." Said Steve

"That is done sir they are disabled." Said the computer

"You are naughty Steve." Said Lydia with a smile

"I really do not have the time for their nonsense." Said Steve as he pulled back close to her parent's house.

"Computer scans the house for any life signs and any danger." Said Steve

Lydia looked at Steve with surprise.

"It is just a formality my love, I can not put you in danger at this time." Said Steve when he saw her concern

"There are two people in the house and they seem to be sleeping." Said the computer

"Are they still alive?" ask Steve

"Yes they are one of them just got up and are walking through the house." Said the computer

Steve moved forward and landed on the lawn next to the house.

"Computer stay on high alert and camouflage your self from the air, I do not want the air police to spot you." Said Steve

"That is done sir." Said the computer

Steve helped Lydia out of the craft and together they went to the front door.

Lydia knocked on the door and her mom came to open up

Her mom got a fright when she saw Lydia and screamed at her husband to come and looked who came home, she held Lydia and won't to leave her for a moment totally ignored Steve.

Her dad came into the room and saw Lydia and Steve, he shook hands with Steve and then kissed Lydia softly.

"What brings you by commander?" ask her dad

"It is now Admiral Dad." Said Lydia

"Oh sorry sir I did not notice." Said her dad

"We are on our way back to the academy and wanted to collect her son as we got married this morning and are a family now." Said Steve

"Married, but that is fantastic news." Said her dad

The two woman were so involved talking that the mother did not hear a word Steve were saying, her mom had her ear on Lydia's stomach and screech with laugher when the baby moved.

Steve decided it is time to get control over the situation

"Let us go and sit down as there are some things that we need to discuss." Said Steve loud and clear so that the woman can hear him.

They sat down and both the parents got his attention now.

"Now mom and dad as you know Lydia and I got married today and am leaving to our home planet to commence on our new duties at the academy." Said Steve

"Isn't it wonderful." Said her mom

"I did not have a moment to discuss this with Lydia yet as things are hectic in space at the moment, but her son has to come with us, as we are a family now." Said Steve

"Oh no I am going to miss him so much we love that little boy." said her mom

"If you give me a moment you will not miss him at all." Said Steve

"How do you mean, not miss him at all?" ask Lydia

"The house we are moving to have a three bedroom flat joint to the house with its own entrance and shuttle bay. If your parents agree to it then they could come with us to live there in the flat and be with you all the time." Said Steve

There was a shocked silence

"But how do we get there, we do not have transport?" said her dad

"No problem we just pack your stuff, transport it to our ship and you travel with us." Said Steve

"Mom that will be fantastic, please come with us?" ask Lydia

"Your mom and dad needs to make a decision together love, so let them talk it through." Said Steve

"I will give everything to be with my child and grand children." Said her mom

"That is fine we will come with you, this place we moved to years ago was just because I had to for my retirement, and I don't mind moving again." Says her dad

"Good, Lydia you and your mom must go and fetch your son I think he will be delighted to see you again, your dad and I will start the logistics of the move." Said Steve.

A short wile later the two woman and the boy came back to find Steve and her dad sitting on the veranda having a drink and dad smoking a cigar.

With her hands on her hips, Lydia frowns and commented

"Is that how you discuss logistics Admiral?" ask Lydia

"It is all done already my dear wife, storage bags have been transferred from the ship to us here, they are in the sitting room, all we have to do is to pack every thing into them and transfer. While you do the packing we will give all the furniture a code so that that could be transferred as well." Said Steve with a smile

"All worked out hey." Said Lydia.

"Yes the faster we pack the faster we get going." Said Steve

"How long before the ship is out of transport range?" ask her dad

"Dad, two days will be fine three days will be risky." Said Steve

"We better get going then." Said her dad

Steve started to give the furniture codes and her dad assist by selecting what must go and what must stay.

"Some of these furniture is really old, I would like to replace some of them if that is at all possible." Said her dad

"Anything is possible, I tell you what, leave behind all the furniture that does not have any material value to you, then we will replace them as soon as we get there." Said Steve

"That is a brilliant idea, let us leave all the furniture behind, I feel a change is good for us at our age." Said her dad

"Love we are replacing all the furniture on the other side, is that fine with you." Shout her dad.

"Why do you want to do that for?" ask her mom shocked.

"Because we deserve it, we gave our lives for the fleet and our planets and the Admiral said he will arrange that." Said her dad

Steve knew the old man was lying, he did not say it like that, but he will have to do it to keep the peace and to get going.

"Aright then leave it all, we are almost packed here. Said her mom.

Lydia gave Steve a look seeking conformation, he just nodded his head in agreement, and she smiled silently and continues packing.

A wile later everything was packed and Steve contacted the ship.
"Dex the bags are ready for transport, please transport now." Said Steve
"Transporting now sir." Said Dex
The bags disappear into thin air in front of them.
"Transport complete sir." Said Dex
"Thank you we are on our way." Said Steve and broke contact.

Lydia is holding her son on her lap as Steve got into his craft.
"Lydia, I think your son must rather sit here in front with me so that he can see what I am doing, it will be better for your unborn child." Said Steve
"You right." Said Lydia
"Do you want to sit in front by that nice gentlemen?" ask Lydia her son
"Yes mom, I want to see if he does something wrong, then I will moan with him." Said the boy.
"You are going to moan a lot." Said Lydia with a smile
They took of and Steve really opened the throttle wide and shot out to space. In a few seconds they were in space and Steve turned the craft into the direction of the mother ship.
"Wow, that was amazing, I never experience such a lift off before, what speed are we doing now?" ask her dad
"We are traveling at three light years an hour at the moment but will increase speed soon." Said Steve
"But now I don't understand. The maximum speed for any craft in the fleet is only two and a half light years an hour, and you are already at three

and is going to go faster, how is that possible?" ask her dad now very curiously.

Steve has actually forgotten that the old man is an engineer.

"I will explain that to you a bit later, no craft in the fleet can go this fast except mine, I have played with it a bit and is still testing it, so by the way sir, how does it feel to travel at four times the speed of light, as that is what we are doing at the moment?" ask Steve

"That is impossible, let me see the speed dial." Said her dad

Steve let him come forward, he just whistles, and tap Steve on the shoulder.

"Well done Admiral, I never thought I will live to see that day, and now I am traveling at that speed. I can die now so happy I am." Said her dad

"No dad you must not die now, you must see what else my husband constructed to win this war." Said Lydia

"What else has he done, come tell me my child I want to know everything?" ask her dad

"Dad, we will have lots of time to show you once we are on the ship, so sit back and enjoy the ride." Said Steve

"Oh I am enjoying it ,oh yes I am." Said her dad

A little later Steve tap on the speed dial and softly showed the boy to keep this a secret, the speed was five light years an hour, the boy held his hand in front of his mouth as not to speak and shook his head in agreement, looking at grand pa and softly giggle.

Steve saw the mother ship on the radar and closed the speed valves.

"Dex what it your speed at the moment?" ask Steve

"Two light years an hour sir, we are holding back for you sir." Said Dex

"I want you to increase your speed to three light years, I am coming from behind and am going to overshoot on the right hand side of you." Said Steve

"I will be on the look out for you sir." Said Dex
Steve went past the mother ship at four light years an hour. Then applied space brakes and turned into a sharp turn to end up behind the ship again.
Steve marched the speed of the mother ship and docked without any problems.
"Now that is what I call flying." Said her dad as they disembarked from the craft.

"I am glad that dad witnesses the flying skills of my husband, you should see him shooting the enemy down dad, and this man is amazing." Boost Lydia
"It looks that way, you made the right decision to marry him." Said her dad smiling
Dex met up with them and showed her mom and dad their new quarters and their new home for the next two months.

When Lydia got to her quarters she found that her belongongs has been moved to Steve's quarters and neatly packed away into the cupboards. She felt very tired after a long day and is still dressed in the dress that she got married in, and so is Steve. She wonders where he is.
Lydia decided to take a shower and to get some rest as the baby needs the rest more than anything. She was in the shower when Steve came in.
"Where were you?" ask Lydia

"Sorry my love I had to go to the bridge, the admiral wanted some documents signed for your parents to be on board, that is standard protocol when civilians travel with the fleet.." said Steve

"Get yourself out of those clothes and come and wash my back." Ordered Lydia

"Yes my love anytime, how are you feeling?" ask Steve

"Tired, I need some rest badly." Said Lydia

"I will not disturb you to much then." Said Steve as he got in the shower with her.

Steve woke up with his buzzer going of, it was the bridge, and he is needed.

Steve got dressed and went to the bridge, Lydia did not wake up when he left.

"What is wrong Dex?" ask Steve

"There is a group of ships stationed thirty light years from here, the front ships picked them up and stopped the whole fleet, sir." Said Dex

"Can they identify these ships?" ask Steve

"No they can not, the Admiral called for caution, and he said that you must handle it, just incase it is still from the enemy forces that were running." Said Dex

"Transfer two destroyers to their location but program them not to fire but to sent photos of these ships so that we can decide what action to take." Said Steve

"That will be done sir, shall we use some of the ones in our cargo bay sir?" ask Dex

"Yes we do not want to leave the other ships without first line defense." Said Steve

The destroyers were sent and the photos came back.

Six hips belong to a friendly planet close to their home, two ships were from our fleet and five ships were from the academy that was used to train the pilots in space.

"Open the channel to the ships of the fleet?" ask Steve

"This is Admiral Holt you are within range, what is your purpose so far from home?" ask Steve

"We came to escort you home Admiral, all of you are heroes, and the fleet sent us to bring you in." said the voice.

"Very well then." Said Steve

"Dex sent a signal that they are from the fleet and here to escort we home." Said Steve

The convoy started moving again and Steve went back to his quarters where his new life is waiting for him.

He found her still sleeping and he got into bed with her and held has softly as to not wake her up.

Thoughts went through his mind, how are it going to be with them working together, the new baby, and her parents close by.

Steve gives a smile in the darkness of the room, this is what he wanted for him self and he was happy, not only for himself but also for Lydia, together they will now have a great live together, and they are going to enjoy every moment of it.

The next week that followed Steve and the old man really start to know each other, her dad was an interesting man with a keen interest at the new technology in engineering.

Whenever Steve looked for him, he is found in engineering, but the engineer's love him down there as he always has good stories to tell and interesting things that he designed at his time.

That gave Steve a thought.

"Sir would you like to build something with me at engineering?" ask Steve

"I will be delighted sir, what do you have in mind?" ask her dad

"I am not going to tell you, it is a secret." Said Steve with a smile

"Oh I love secrets, let us go Admiral." Said her dad

They went to engineering and Steve got some pipes out of the store and started to build cooling fans with fins into it to cool down the core.

The old man helped Steve with the welding and cutting of the steel while Steve worked on some electronic pc boards, which the old man did not understand.

For three days they were working with him not knowing what they were doing.

When the task was complete, Steve connected the cooling fins to the core and the temperature dropped right down.

"Now sir let us go to the bridge." Said Steve

"I am right behind you sir." Said her dad

On the bridge Steve increased the ships space awareness with fifty percent and then removed the throttle of the ship's control box, and then he connected the electronic board he constructed into the throttle body and placed it back into position.

"Helmsman, what is your throttle position now reading?" ask Steve

"It only reads twenty five percent sir, I do not understand it sir we are traveling at maximum speed of two and a half light years an hour sir." Said the helmsman

"That is ok, now go a half light year to the starboard side and let me know when you are there?" ask Steve

"I will confirm sir." Said the helmsman

Steve took out the ships awareness control and did some settings to the unit; the star map now is showing much further into space than before, way past the front ship.

"I confirm that we are in position sir." Said the helmsman.

The Admiral came on line.

"Steve what is going on, you change direction and is now far out?" ask the Admiral

"I am just doing some test sir, not to worry sir." Said Steve

"Very well then, I will not ask questions as I am scared of the answer." Said the Admiral

Steve just smiled

"Helmsman. Throttle up to the half way mark." Said Steve

"Done sir, the ship is now traveling at four light years sir." Said the helmsman

"Good increase speed to the three quarter mark." Said Steve

Steve could see the hesitation in the man

"Steve what are you doing, you are leaving us behind?" ask the Admiral

"Just testing sir I will be back." Said Steve

"On the mark sir." Said the helmsman

"What speed are we doing now?" asked Steve

"Five light years an hour sir." Said the helmsman.

"Hold it there." Said Steve

The old man found himself a chair; he could not believe what he is experiencing.

"Admiral we are traveling at five light years an hour, with the throttle in the seventy five percent marks. I will not push it any further, all systems are normal." Said Steve

"That is fantastic Steve, can you upgrade the fleet like that?" ask the Admiral

"Yes sir the plans will be sent to the fleet and engineering can go ahead sir." Said Steve

"Good we will save six weeks traveling time with this new speed." Said the Admiral

Lydia came to the bridge and stood next to Steve

"Admiral you must not travel at these speeds, just now the baby gets borne with a beard." Said her dad.

Every one on the bridge started laughing at the remark

Steve sent the plans to the fleet and they started to upgrade the system.

"Sir would you like to go to each ship and see if they are doing it correctly as you now knows how it works?" ask Steve the old man

"It would be my pleasure Admiral." Said her dad and left much exited that he could do something for the fleet.

One week later all the ships in the fleet landed at the academy, six weeks early, but not one crew member complained as they were all on leave for six months.

Steve and Lydia stood in front of their new home and Steve put his hands around her.

"This my lady is the beginning of a new life for us, I think we will be very happy here." said Steve

"I could not wish for a better life than with you, I do not care where it is, but this is excellent. I love you very much and do not want this happiness ever to end." Said Lydia stroking her stomach.

The end.